Mystery of Sebastian Island

Mystery of Sebastian Island

Margaret Goff Clark

DODD, MEAD & COMPANY

NEW YORK

Map on page 10 by Salem Tamer

2 3 4 5 6 7 8 9 10

To MAYNARD and FLORENCE
with thanks for making the world
a safer and friendlier place
for all whose lives have touched theirs

I should like to thank John and Paul, both Special Agents of the USDEA, for all their help and for reading the manuscript.

Also, I am grateful to John and Gladys Mitchell and Anne Kuhn, friends on a certain island.

MGC

Contents

You will find Sebastian Island only in this book. It is made of pieces of many islands, assembled by the author.

1

Blue-eyed Stranger

When Dena Foster entered the Harbor Coffee Shop at 5:00 P.M. it was almost empty.

The door clicked shut behind her. It nipped off the sound of traffic and the screams of the gulls that flew over Gullport Harbor across the street and closed her into a different world, a world of air-conditioned cool and the scent of coffee and hot grease.

Dena found a table against the wall and for a moment sat perfectly still. The air in the coffee shop was refreshing after the heat outdoors. Already her short, blonde hair felt cool and damp against the nape of her neck. June on the far northern coast of Maine was rarely as hot as today.

Dena picked up the menu. It was early for dinner, but she was hungry after the long ride from boarding school. She was all alone so she could eat whenever and whatever she wished.

She had ordered a cheeseburger and apple pie with ice cream when the front door opened and a boy came in carrying a dark blue canvas bag zipped across the top like a gym bag. He paused to look around and then walked to a stool at the counter almost directly opposite Dena. She couldn't help noticing his blue eyes and thick, dark hair. Sixteen, Dena decided, about a year older than she. With his dungarees and cotton knit shirt, he was like all of the high-school boys, but something about the way he walked and the way he held his head set him apart. Style. He had style.

Now his back was toward her. Dena watched him set the dark blue bag on the empty seat on his right.

The coffee shop began to fill up. The boy at the counter moved his bag to the floor and a bald-headed man with a fringe of blond hair sat down on the stool. He, too, was carrying a bag which he put on the floor next to the boy's.

How about that? thought Dena. Both bags were dark blue. In fact, they looked exactly alike.

The cheeseburger was good. She was finishing the last bite when the bald man tossed some coins onto the counter to pay for his coffee. He reached down. His fingers closed around the handle of one of the dark blue bags, but it wasn't his bag. It was the one next to the boy.

He swung around on the stool and walked toward the door.

Dena jumped up, jarring the table so that her glass of water splashed over. She ran across to the boy at the counter. "Ex-excuse me," she stammered. "He took your bag. That man. He picked up the wrong bag."

The boy looked up at her with a startled expression in his alert blue eyes. Then he glanced at the floor. "No, he didn't, Miss. There's my bag."

"But it isn't yours. His was just like it." Dena was becoming more and more concerned. She sent an anxious glance toward the door. Already the man was outside. Her voice rose excitedly. "If you don't stop him it'll be too late!"

Heads were turning toward her, but she was too absorbed to notice. "Look in it!" she begged.

The boy picked up the bag, but he didn't open it. "This is mine, all right. Thanks a lot for trying to help." He set the bag on the floor again and took up his hamburger. His face was red.

Dena still did not leave. How could she make him understand?

"It's OK," he assured her again, and deliberately turned his back.

I'm making a fool of myself, thought Dena, suddenly aware of the staring eyes of the other customers. She slunk back to her seat wishing she were invisible.

The waitress brought her apple pie with ice cream. Dena ate it because she didn't want to waste it, but she had no idea how it tasted. She kept thinking, I *know* that man got the wrong bag! Why didn't the boy look to be sure he had the right one? Tonight, or whenever he did look inside, he'd be sorry.

What was inside his bag? she wondered. Gym shoes and dirty, smelly towels? Was that why he didn't want to open it in the restaurant?

As soon as the waitress brought the bill, Dena paid it and left.

The sun was still high and although it was now six o'clock, the air outside remained warmer than in the coffee shop. Dena crossed the street and threaded her way through a parking lot to the waterfront.

She walked to the end of the public wharf and leaned on one of the posts, taking deep breaths of the fresh sea air.

As usual, the gulls were swinging and diving over the harbor like paper airplanes. A lobster boat was coming in after a day of hauling, and nearby a cormorant sat on a piling, a black-robed witch with wings instead of a broomstick.

Across a narrow strip of water, at the end of the next dock, was the *Henrietta*, the little mailboat that tomorrow would carry her to Sebastian Island, eighteen miles into the Atlantic Ocean.

Dena had mixed feelings when she looked at the *Henrietta*. Of course she was glad school was over and she was going home. But home wouldn't be the same as before. Her new stepfather would be on hand as he had been during spring vacation. He'd be out in his lobster boat part of the time, but when he was home he'd be telling her what she could do and what she couldn't.

Her own father had been washed off his lobster boat and drowned during a storm when Dena was seven. Even after eight years she wasn't ready to accept another man in his place. Her father had been a real lobsterman, Dena thought proudly. Paul just worked at it part time, when he wasn't teaching school.

For her mother's sake she'd try not to show how she hated her stepfather. It wouldn't be easy. How could she be expected to like someone who didn't want her around? He was the one who had said she must spend the past year at a boarding school when she should've been in school in Gullport with the rest of her friends from Sebastian Island. She couldn't forgive him for that.

Well, at least she had tonight. Dena closed her mind to the next day's problems. Tonight she had a room in the motel across the street and she was on her own. A motel room alone, right in town. What luxury! And it would be so easy in the morning to walk across the street and board the *Henrietta*.

She had caught a ride to Gullport with a girl from school who lived in New Brunswick, and the bus money she had saved had more than paid for the room. She hoped her mother wouldn't mind. After all, there wasn't a boat until tomorrow.

Being alone gave Dena a delicious sense of freedom, a foretaste of more freedom to come in a few years. She knew she was going to like being grown up, old enough to get a job and go to some strange city to live. Let the time go quickly until then!

Her evening of freedom went by too fast. She started with an hour of shopping in the stores that stocked beautiful wares for tourists. After that she found a coffee shop where teens gathered to talk and listen to music.

Dena boarded the *Henrietta* at seven-forty the next morning, twenty minutes before sailing time. It was a dull day with no wind here in the sheltered harbor. The water was like pale gray silk.

With her back against the railing in the bow, Dena watched the few other passengers come down the gangplank. She hoped to recognize someone from Sebastian Island, but she saw only strangers.

Well, Maryann had warned her. Maryann Kosac had been her best friend on the island. Only a month ago she had moved away.

"Things are different on Sebastian," she had written. "Several city people have bought houses there and new people own the store and lobster car. The islanders don't mix with them any more than they have to. They're not our kind. They have stacks of money!

"Dad got such a good offer for our place he said he couldn't pass it up. I'm going to miss the island, and you most of all."

The Kosacs lived in Boston now. Dena knew she'd

be lonely without Maryann.

Suddenly she came out of her daydream. Striding down the gangplank was the boy she had seen in the Harbor Coffee Shop the night before. He was carrying the dark blue canvas bag.

2

The Missing Lobster Buoys

The boy added his bag to the mound of luggage and supplies piled on the forward deck. Without a glance in her direction he went behind the cabin.

Had he seen her and decided to stay out of sight so she wouldn't embarrass him again? Dena reddened at the memory of the scene in the coffee shop.

Why do I do things like that? she wondered. I don't even think. I just spring into action if I believe I can help. I'm always barging in.

Dena turned around and stared at the busy harbor. A sailboat pulled anchor nearby and started out under the power of its motor, the sails still tightly rolled. At the next wharf a lobsterman was hoisting a drum of fish scraps into his boat. He'd use them for baiting his traps.

"Hi!"

Dena whirled around to meet a pair of laughing blue eyes. It was the boy from the coffee shop.

"Here we are again," he said. "Guess the stars or fate or something have thrown us together." He held out his hand. "Guy O'Neill."

The twinkle in his eyes was infectious. Dena had to smile as she shook hands with him and introduced herself. She had made up her mind she would never again mention that crazy bag, but the words popped out. "Did you have your own bag?"

"Yes."

"I still don't see. I'm sorry I made such a fuss."

"Forget it. You meant well."

Dena groaned. "I hate people who mean well, but make pests of themselves."

Guy ignored this remark. "Dena Foster. I think I know your stepfather. Paul Roth. Right?"

"How did you know?"

"I live on the same road you do. My uncle bought the Nelson place last fall. I stay with him and my aunt but I've been away in school until two days ago."

"Me, too. I mean I've been at boarding school over in the southwestern part of the state. I'm just on my way home now," said Dena.

"Then you're in high school?" asked Guy.

"Tenth grade this fall."

"I'll be a junior. You going to stay home all summer?"

"Yes."

"Great!"

Dena was surprised at the warmth of his tone. She wasn't accustomed to attention from boys, especially boys like Guy, good-looking fellows who knew their way around. In fact, she had known few boys outside of the handful on the island and she knew them so well they seemed like brothers. This past year she had been in an all-girl school.

Guy looked away, toward the rear of the boat. "I have a friend back there waiting for me. Why don't you come along? There's a bench behind the cabin."

"Thanks. Maybe later." Dena felt shy about joining Guy and his friend. They'd have things they'd like to talk about together. She'd be in the way. Besides, she liked to ride in the bow where she could look ahead and see everything and feel the wind blowing her hair.

Guy started away, then stopped and added, "See you." He made it sound like a promise.

Dena watched him until he was out of sight.

The ship's bell clanged. A man on the dock cast off the last mooring line.

Running footsteps sounded on the wharf. A tall, sandy-haired boy in jeans and windbreaker was racing toward the *Henrietta*. He was balancing a duffel bag on his shoulder and carrying a guitar.

"Hurry, Barney!" shouted Dena.

Barney Sebastian always spent part of the summer on Sebastian Island with his grandfather. He and Dena had been playmates since they were eight.

The gangplank had already been taken in, but Barney didn't pause. He flew over the widening gap like an Olympic broadjumper.

Several people on board applauded.

He gave a mock bow, hampered by his burdens. Then he started toward Dena.

She ran to meet him, ready to throw her arms around his neck as she had last year, but a few paces away she stopped. He looked so much older than he had last summer, and she had to look up to meet his eyes. For the first time in her life she felt self-conscious with her old friend.

But Barney dropped his duffel bag, set down the guitar, and wrapped his long arms around her. He gave her a hearty kiss.

"Hey, Shrimp!" he teased, holding her off and looking her up and down. "I thought you and I were the same size."

She stood as tall as possible. "I may be shorter than you, but don't get the idea you can push me around!"

"Just as tough as ever," he said admiringly. "Hey, you got your hair cut. I like it. Gives you a streamlined look."

The *Henrietta* nosed out toward open water, her sturdy engine vibrating the deck. The boat rose and fell in a gentle rocking motion. Dena's pulse quickened to the beat of the engine. Going home, going home!

Barney improvised a bench from two cartons of canned soup backed by his duffel bag. He always knew how to make the best of a situation, thought

Dena, settling contentedly beside him.

"You're going to have me underfoot all summer," Barney said. "Gramp needs me to help with the lobstering. And he'd rather not be alone."

"I know," said Dena. "Mother told me your grandmother died last winter. I'm sorry. Your grandfather must miss her an awful lot. I haven't seen him since it happened. I haven't been home to the island since September."

"How come?" asked Barney.

"I've been in boarding school."

"What about vacations?"

"We stayed at the apartment outside Gullport." Dena looked away, toward the bow of the *Henrietta* where a dog lay sound asleep on his master's jacket. "My stepfather went over to Sebastian to do some lobstering part of spring vacation, but Mom and I didn't go. The weather was foul."

"So you've been away from the island almost as long as I have," said Barney. "I'm sure glad I'm going back to be with Gramp this summer. I guess he doesn't even eat right, now that he's alone. And he's upset about something else, too." Barney stopped abruptly.

"Like what?" prompted Dena.

Barney didn't answer. Instead he stood up and turned around in a leisurely circle, looking in all directions. When he sat down he spoke softly as if afraid of being overheard.

"Someone has been playing tricks on him."

Dena was startled. "What kind of tricks?"

"The latest was someone stole a lot of buoys off his trap lines."

"That could've been an accident. Was there a storm? Sometimes buoys break loose in a big storm."

"No storm."

Dena shook her head. "That's bad." As a lobsterman's daughter, she understood. She could imagine Gramp Sebastian going out to haul the traps he had set a day or so before and finding only empty ocean where the floating buoys should have marked the location of the traps. Without the buoys it would be difficult to find his expensive lobster traps. Some of them might be lost for good at the bottom of the ocean, filled with lobsters he could never harvest.

"Who'd do a thing like that? I don't know anyone on Sebastian Island who'd pull a trick like that." She remembered Maryann's letter. "But I hear there are some new people on the island. Maybe some of them . . ."

Barney pushed back his hair. The wind had turned it into a lion's mane. "Gramp doesn't think it's any of the new people. He doesn't think they belong on the island, that's for sure, but he says they're rich and wouldn't have any reason for messing around with a lobsterman."

"Does he have any idea who it is? Or why?"

Again Barney stood up and looked around. "Come

23

on. I'm tired of sitting." He pulled Dena to her feet and led the way to the rail. "This'll do," he said.

They leaned elbow to elbow on the rail and Barney continued, "Gramp wrote and said he had an idea but he wasn't going to put it in a letter and maybe have it opened before it ever left the island. That gives you an idea how suspicious he is."

"Yeah. Well, let me know when you find out what he thinks. Barney . . ."

"What?"

"You said the new people are rich. My stepfather's a new person on the island, but you couldn't call him rich."

Barney grinned. "He's in a special class. You know why he's there. Because of your mother. What's he like, anyway?"

Dena kept her eyes on a point of land topped with a sawtooth crown of dark-green pine trees. "He's OK, I guess. His name's Paul Roth and he says I should call him Paul. He's a high-school teacher— same school as Mom. That's how they got acquainted. They got married in August. I wrote you about that."

"I thought you said he was a lobsterman," said Barney.

"He hauls traps when he isn't teaching school," Dena explained. "All summer, of course. And weekends in the spring and fall he and Mom go over to the island and he goes out with his boat. He told me he

24

started lobstering summers when he was in college." She wrinkled her nose. "Curly red hair and a beard."

"Hey, real cool!"

Dena didn't answer. Corny, she was thinking. Paul was trying to look like one of his students. Though Mom had said he was a good teacher—interested in the kids and all that.

"Anyway," said Barney. "I'm supposed to keep my eyes open and try to find out who's sabotaging Gramp and why."

"Sounds like a big job. I'll help."

But how? she wondered. How could you catch a person who went around stealing lobster traps? He must do it at night when no one could see him. But then how could he see the buoys?

Barney nudged her with his elbow. "Look at the guillemots." He pointed to several black duck-like birds with white wing patches. One of them dived, showing its red feet as it went under water for a fish.

"I haven't seen any of them for ages!" It was a relief to get away from thoughts of mean tricks. The familiar birds reminded Dena of the beauties of her island home. She thought of the spruce woods behind the house and the wide sand beach behind that. The strawberries would be ripe in the meadows now and the wild roses would be filling the air with their scent.

Every morning she would wake up in her room at the top of the house and see the waves roll against the

rocks and into the sandy bays. She would listen to
their thunder on stormy nights. . . .

She turned to Barney. "I'm so glad I'm going
home!"

3

The Tower Room

The trip to Sebastian Island took more than two hours, but Dena and Barney talked the whole way.

Once Guy O'Neill came onto the forward deck. Dena motioned to him, but he waved and circled back around the cabin again. He had seen Barney and didn't want to butt in, Dena thought.

Beyond the last sheltering arms of land the sea was no longer calm. Here there was always a wind. The sun had come out and was sparkling on the water that had changed from gray to blue.

Barney looked at his watch. "Half an hour to go." He grinned. "I suppose Gramp will be at the wharf with his wheelbarrow ready to carry my duffel."

"Nobody'll be meeting me," Dena said moodily. "They don't know I'm coming."

"How's that?"

"Oh, I caught a ride with a girl from school. I stayed overnight in a motel. Thought I'd surprise Mom."

Was that it? she wondered. Or hadn't she called

because Paul had made such a point of it? He and Mom would meet her bus, he'd said on the phone. And they'd all go out to dinner and spend the night at the rented apartment outside Gullport. They lived on the mainland during the school year because it was too far to travel back and forth from the island. Dena was annoyed that Paul planned to make all that fuss over her coming home. She knew how he really felt.

"There it is!" Barney pointed ahead to a green mound rising out of the sea.

Dena heard the excitement in his voice and knew he loved the island, too.

Gradually the mound took shape, became high in the center and low and flat in the far south, like a lobsterman's cap with a visor. The spruce and pine woods in the middle of the island were in dark contrast to the sunny meadows and beaches that bordered the water. Rocky arms reached out from the shore, forming protected coves.

The *Henrietta* rounded the end of the sea wall and chugged into West Harbor in the center of the west shore. Dena inhaled contentedly, enjoying the fishy smell and the faint scent of spruce and pine.

Everything looked the same, she noted. The fishhouses still lined the harbor, some of them red with white trim and others with silvery walls that had never tasted paint.

At a distance the people on the wharf blurred together like figures in some modern paintings Dena had seen. Gradually they separated, became heads on top of bodies, then recognizable people.

Dena searched for her mother's face. Of course she didn't know her daughter was coming but she might be on the wharf, like most of the other people on the island, just to see what and who came in on the *Henrietta*. The arrival of the mailboat three times a week was the island's big social event.

Almost every face on the dock was familiar. You didn't live on a little island like Sebastian all your life without getting to know everybody on it. On the whole island there were only about sixty people. Hands were waving and she could hear her name being called. How wonderful to be coming home to your own island!

The *Henrietta* sidled up to the wharf.

Guy O'Neill was at the rail, waiting for the gangplank. He was the first one off the boat.

"Hey, Dena, where's your luggage?" asked Barney. "I just hired out as your porter."

"Forget it. You have enough of your own. I can manage." Her suitcases were heavy, but she had gotten them to the boat, and if she had to, she could carry them the half mile to her home. She didn't want to be a bother to Barney or anyone else.

He shrugged. "OK. Be independent. See you on shore." Barney snatched up his duffel and guitar and, by-passing the crowd, stepped over the rail onto the wharf.

Dena lost sight of him in the crowd. As soon as she left the boat, hands reached out to her and she was hugged and kissed all the way to shore by school friends and older people she had known all her life.

Barney and his grandfather were waiting for her at the end of the wharf. Gramp Sebastian was a broad-shouldered man with curly gray hair and a kindly face that showed he had spent most of his life out-doors. His skin was browned by the sun and wind, and he had a spray of lines in the corners of his eyes from squinting across the water and from smiling. He was a sturdy descendant of the Sebastians who had settled the island two hundred years before.

Gramp was smiling now as Dena approached them.

"Here's my girl," he said in his quiet way. He put his arms around her in a warm fatherly hug, then held her away at arm's length to study her face. "Prettier than ever."

Dena reddened. "Thank you, Mr. Sebastian."

"What's this Mr. Sebastian? You getting too old to call me Gramp?" He set her suitcases in the empty wheelbarrow. "Come on. We'll take you home. We're leaving Barney's gear under the tree till we come back."

She could see there was no use arguing with Gramp. "Thanks so much. Those bags weigh a ton."

"I agree," he said. "You sure must have a lot of clothes."

"And books. One of those suitcases is full of books."

Barney pushed the wheelbarrow up the hill toward the store. "That sure was some welcome you got when you came in, Dena."

"That's just because I've lived here all my life."

Gramp spoke up. "Don't try to con us. You must've done something right to get all that lovin'. I've always lived here, too, and no one hugs and kisses me when I come home from Gullport."

Suddenly his face went grim and Dena guessed that his own words had reminded him of his loss.

Shyly she took his hand. "I'm sorry about your wife."

He said nothing for a minute or two. When he spoke again his voice was gruff. "We had thirty-nine good years together, and a lot of people don't have that. But I can't seem to get used to . . ." His voice trailed off.

Dena looked across at Barney and saw the sympathy in his eyes. She guessed that he didn't know what to say, any more than she did.

But Gramp's head was up again and his chin had a determined set. "I'm sure glad Barney's here now. If only he could cook!"

As they neared the store a man in black rubber boots called out to Gramp. "I see you're in already. How come you got such an early start today? I can't keep up with you, old man."

"Hi, there!" Gramp called back. "But you're wrong, Sam. I haven't been out yet."

Sam paused. "I didn't see your boat when I went by East Bay about six this A.M."

"Better have your eyes checked," said Gramp. "The *Martha* was there."

Sam went on, shaking his head.

Gramp stared after him. "I wonder. I'd better take a look when I get home."

A short distance past the store they took a tree-lined road to the right. Except for the thickly settled west shore, houses were far apart on the island and they passed none in the half-mile walk to Dena's home.

Dena felt her eyes smart with tears when she first glimpsed the house in the distance, gleaming white above the trees. All she could see was the eight-sided tower room. The tower always reminded Dena of the topmost layer on a wedding cake.

"There's my room," she said blissfully.

"I know," said Barney. "You're lucky. You must have a great view."

"If the earth didn't curve I could see Portugal. There's nothing in the way. My room is the best lookout on Sebastian Island."

4

A Cold Welcome

A crunching of gravel in the road behind them made all three turn around.

A motorized golf cart was approaching rapidly.

How strange to see a golf cart here! thought Dena. There was no golf course on the island. But come to think of it, the little electric vehicle was a good way to get around on an island only a mile and a half long.

Now the cart was near enough so she could recognize the boy in the seat beside the driver. It was Guy O'Neill.

The golf cart halted beside Dena, and Guy called out a friendly, "Hi!"

The driver, a distinguished-looking man with a neat, sand-colored mustache, said, "Hello, Gramp. Can we give you a hand with those suitcases? You can put them in the back." He motioned behind the seat to the space designed to hold golf clubs. It was now occupied only by the small blue bag.

"Thanks, Mr. Kaufman," said Gramp. "But we're almost there."

Mr. Kaufman leaned out and smiled at Dena. "I'm Guy's uncle. Guy told me about you. I know your stepfather well." He turned to Barney. "And you must be Mr. Sebastian's grandson."

Guy's uncle didn't look at all like Guy, thought Dena. He was blond rather than dark-haired and he appeared to be much shorter than his nephew.

While Guy and Barney were being introduced, Dena could feel Guy's uncle watching her, his eyes narrowed. It made her feel uncomfortable. She wondered what he was thinking, but he only said with a smile, "Trust Guy to find a pretty girl."

Dena flushed and avoided looking at Guy. She hoped he wasn't embarrassed. After all, he wouldn't have spoken to her at all if she hadn't gotten so excited about the two gym bags.

The cart started quietly forward. Guy and his uncle waved.

"That was kind of them to offer to help," Dena said to no one in particular.

"I think they stopped to look us over," Barney said bluntly. "Why would we want them to take your suitcases? They could see we were practically at your house."

Gramp chuckled. "You're a cynical kid. Kaufman just wanted to be friendly. That's his way. He's one newcomer who pulls his own weight. I hate to think what our taxes would be if it weren't for Earl Kaufman."

Barney looked puzzled. "What does he have to do with your taxes?"

"Plenty. We have several new families on the island and they brought along their city luxuries—clothes driers and color TV and electric stoves. Our old generator couldn't turn out enough electricity. And then, too, they wanted better roads for their fancy cars."

Dena walked beside Barney, keeping her eyes on the white tower above the trees. She was listening to Gramp, but at the same time part of her mind was thinking, In a few minutes I'll be home!

Gramp was saying, "Our mayor called a meeting for everyone on the island and laid it on the line that we old-time islanders didn't need all those electrical gadgets and we couldn't pay for running them for somebody else.

"That's when Kaufman stood up and said he didn't blame us. He said he'd give ten thousand dollars toward a new generator and fixing the roads. Well, that started the other new people to thinking and one after another they jumped up and pledged a thousand or so until there was enough in the kitty."

"I noticed the roads," said Dena. "Don't you like them?"

Gramp's bushy eyebrows drew together. "Why should I want 'em? Smooth roads mean cars and motorcycles can tear around scaring the birds and what few animals we have."

Barney looked at Dena with a grin. "Gramp wants

to keep everything the way it was a hundred years ago. He still doesn't have electricity." He moaned. "No TV."

Gramp said sharply, "A summer without TV will be good for you. You'll be outdoors all day, and at night you'll be tired enough to go to bed."

They had reached the house. Barney trundled the wheelbarrow up the flower-bordered walk to the porch.

"Doesn't look as if anyone's home," he remarked.

No car was parked in the short driveway. Dena knew that must mean her mother had the old station wagon, for Paul never took it when he went out to haul lobsters. There was no road to East Bay where he kept his boat.

"If no one's here you can come home with us," offered Gramp.

"Thanks. But I can get in. We never lock the door, day or night."

Dena ran up the steps, tripping on the top step in her haste. She crossed the porch and grasped the doorknob, certain that it would turn, but it would not. She tried again.

"It's locked!" she exclaimed. How could it be? she thought with rising irritation. We *never* lock it.

Barney joined her and put a firm thumb on the doorbell. Dena could hear it ringing inside the house.

This is what I get for not phoning, she thought. Nobody's here and I'm locked out of my own home.

Suddenly the door opened and her stepfather appeared, his red hair and beard shining in the dim light of the hallway. He was dressed in his old work shirt and paint-spattered dungarees.

"Hello, there, Dena! Good to see you again." He took her hand and gave her a quick kiss on the cheek. Looking past her at Gramp and Barney, he said, "Hi, Gramp. So this is the fellow you've been expecting."

Paul shook hands with Barney, but he stayed in the doorway. Dena thought, He acts as if we're strangers and he doesn't want to let us in.

Gramp asked, "Where would you like these ten-ton suitcases?"

"Oh, on the porch. I'll take them in." It was plain that Paul's mind was on something else. He looked from Gramp to Dena and then said hesitantly, "We didn't know you were coming home today, Dena, so we made other plans. Your mother went to Gullport yesterday and I can't look after you, either. I'm leaving for the fishhouse to work on my traps. Sea worms have gotten into the wood and some of the traps have to be rebuilt.

Dena said indignantly, "I don't need anyone to look after me."

"No, of course not. But I'm afraid there isn't much in the fridge to eat. Janet's buying some food in Gullport."

Gramp seemed to understand what Paul was suggesting. He said heartily, "Don't worry a minute,

Paul. Dena can come home with us."

Dena was embarrassed. She felt that Paul had put Gramp on the spot. "You don't have to invite me, Gramp. I'm not hungry, anyway." That was a lie, she had to admit to herself. She had had an early, hurried breakfast, and now at almost eleven o'clock she had a hollow feeling in her stomach.

"Dena, maybe you'd like to meet your mother at the airstrip," said Paul. "You won't have far to go from Gramp's place." He seemed to think the matter was settled and she was going home with Gramp and Barney. He rambled on. "Janet will be flying in about two o'clock. The station wagon's at the airstrip, so you'll have a ride back."

Dena clutched her purse and kept her eyes fixed straight ahead. Paul needn't think he could talk her into leaving. Not when she had just gotten home. "I'm going to stay here," she announced.

Paul gave her a quick, impatient look. "Dena, it's much better for you to go home with Gramp. You'd be all alone here."

"I don't care. I've been away from home for a long time. I want to go up to my room and unpack." She felt shaky and her eyes were hot with tears she was determined not to shed. "Gramp, thanks so much. I'd like to come some other time."

Gramp took hold of the handles of the empty wheelbarrow. "Sure, Dena. I know how you feel. That's the way I am after one day in Gullport. Home

looks so good I don't want to stir out of it." He nodded to Paul. "She's a girl who knows her own mind. I
don't think you have to worry about leaving her
alone."

Barney picked up the suitcases that Gramp had set
on the porch. "I'll take these up to Dena's room, Mr.
Roth."

Paul's face looked stormy. But he stepped out of
the doorway so Barney could go through. "Sure.
Thanks. Put them in the last room on your right, second floor."

"Oh, no!" protested Dena. "The tower room is
mine. Did you forget?"

"Sorry, Dena." It was Paul's turn to look embarrassed. "I'm using that room right now. I'm working
on a special project. The tower room seemed the best
place for me."

5

Break-in!

"But it's *my* room!" Dena cried.

She stared at Paul with eyes that were hot with anger. She had never in her life felt so outraged. What made him think he could move in and take her room, the room that had been her private refuge for years?

Paul said, "Let's talk about it later."

Dena didn't want to wait until later. She wanted to settle this now. But Gramp was standing at the foot of the steps and Barney would be down soon. She didn't want to argue with Paul in front of them. In fact, she wouldn't argue at all. She'd wait until her mother came home and let her tell Paul to move out of the tower room.

Barney thudded down the stairs from the second floor. He called out, "See you later!" and joined his grandfather.

" 'Bye!" said Dena. "Thanks for your help."

Then without another word she brushed past Paul and raced up the stairs and down the hall to the room where Barney had left her suitcases. There she kicked off her shoes and flung herself onto the bed and cried.

She heard her stepfather call, "I'm going now, Dena!" Then the back door slammed behind him.

Dena sat up and wiped her eyes. The room was unbearably warm, and no wonder, the windows were closed.

She opened the windows wide and let the breeze from the ocean enter. It flung the thin nylon curtains into the room like white banners in a parade.

Dena stared out, unhappily comparing the view with that from the tower windows. She could see the ocean, but the patch of spruce woods directly behind the house hid the meadow and the cliff above the shore. In the tower room she had felt as if she were floating in a space capsule. Here, she was earthbound.

Disheartened, she turned to study the room that Paul said was hers.

At once she recognized the blue bedspread from the tower room. Her chair with its matching blue slipcover was here, also. Both slipcover and spread had been freshly laundered. The bookcase was stocked with her own books and standing beside it was her desk topped with a new green blotter.

All of these mute objects seemed to be speaking to her. They made it clear that Mom had agreed to let Paul take over the tower room.

Dena wanted to cry again, but instead, still barefooted, she hurried out of the room and down the hall to the stairs that rose steeply from the center of the second floor. Quickly she climbed them and pulled open the door to the tower.

The beige monk's cloth drapes had been pulled back so the sunlight sparkled on the floor and walls. How bare the room looked! All of her furniture was gone except for the bed and that was covered with a plain brown spread. A table against the north wall bore a typewriter, a stack of white paper, and several books.

What was Paul working on that he needed this room? The typewriter and paper suggested that he might be writing a book, but why couldn't he do that in the study downstairs?

Her eyes darted around the room, searching for clues. A shiny object on the padded seat under the east windows caught her attention. She went closer and picked it up. An old spyglass. Her spyglass.

It had belonged to a great-great-grandmother whose husband was a whaler. Dena could imagine her at the window, peering at every ship.

She herself had used the glass to search for her father's boat coming in from lobstering and, when she was older, to study the stars.

What was Paul doing with it? Was this a clue as to why he wanted this room? Dena crossed to the table and looked at the titles of the books that were piled there. All were about birds. That must be it, then.

He was writing a book about birds and he was watching them from this room.

That seemed odd. He could see the birds better if he walked in the fields and woods and studied them close at hand.

Dena knelt on the window seat to gaze out at the Atlantic, remembering a day long ago, one of the first times she had come to this room.

It was her seventh birthday. Her father, her very own father, had taken her up to the tower in the morning.

"What do you think of this room, Dena?" he had asked. He led her to the windows that looked toward the east. It had been a bright day then as now and she could see far out on the water where the smoke from a big ocean liner looked like the tail of a cat against the sky. The ship was so far away, that was all she could see, just the smoke.

Dena had followed her father from one window to the next, more and more fascinated by the different views.

Then her father had said, "See the shelves under these windows? They'd be a good place for your books and dolls. And here's a window seat with a cushion. Think about it, Dena. Would you like this room for your own?"

She had thrown her arms around him in rapture. "Oh, yes, yes! Bring my bed up now!"

It had been her room ever since, and she had loved

43

it every minute of the eight years since she had moved into it.

Dena sat down on the window seat and surveyed the empty bookshelves. How *could* Mom let Paul take this room? What was he doing here?

She resisted an impulse to go to the table to examine what had been written on the paper. She had begun to realize that no matter how she felt about it, this room was now Paul's.

I might as well go down and unpack my suitcases, she thought.

But first she would go to the kitchen and find something to eat. At least she could have a peanut-butter sandwich. No matter what Paul said, Mom always kept enough food in the house for a mug-up.

She hadn't thought of that expression for a long time. She wondered if Guy would know that mug-up meant a snack or a light lunch.

She had reached the top of the stairs on the second floor when a sound made her pause and listen. Someone was turning the handle on the back door. A neighbor? But a neighbor would knock or ring the bell.

Had Paul returned for something he had forgotten? But if so, why would it take him so long to come in? Even if the door was locked, he'd have the key.

The sound of the doorknob being turned stopped. Dena had started slowly down the steps when she heard a different sound. It was a faint scratching noise of metal on metal. Then the door opened and closed.

So it must be Paul. Why didn't he call out and let her know he was home?

She opened her mouth to shout, "Paul?" But before the word came out, she heard heavy footsteps run from the kitchen, across the dining room, and into the study.

Dena froze. Those were not Paul's footsteps! Someone was in the study, someone who had no right to be there.

Her thoughts rushed frantically this way and that. What did he want? He couldn't expect to find much money or anything valuable in this house. He was taking an awful chance breaking in by daylight. Had he been watching so he knew her mother and Paul had gone out?

A shiver ran down Dena's backbone. Perhaps he knew she had arrived and that she was alone in the house!

Dena clung to the railing as if it were a life line. She wondered if she should go back to the tower room and hope the intruder would go away. Or should she make a dash for the front door? If she went outside he might run after her and catch her. There was no house nearby where she could go for help.

But if she returned to the tower and he came up she'd be trapped for sure.

Dena wished fervently for an upstairs telephone. She had wanted one in her room for a long time, but Mom always said it was too expensive to have an extension. The only phone was in the study off the dining room and that's where *he* was. Her only hope was to get out of the house.

Anyway, she thought, if she did call the constable he'd be out in his lobster boat this time of day. Sebastian Island wasn't well equipped to fight crime because the people on it had always been law-abiding.

Again she started cautiously down, her bare feet making no sound on the stairs.

Halfway down was a landing where the steps made a right-angle turn to go into the living room. From that point on she would be in full view of anyone in the living room or dining area, which was only an ell of the living room. But she wouldn't be able to see *him* until her eyes were below the level of the first floor ceiling.

Dena stopped at the landing and listened. She heard no sound except for the thump of her own heart. The front door, ten feet beyond the foot of the stairs, looked impossibly distant, but she had to get there.

With her back pressed against the outside wall, she started down the last flight of stairs.

6

The Intruder Vanishes

When Dena left the landing the rooms below were quiet. But as her foot came down on the third step she heard a crash in the study. This was followed by scurrying footsteps that fled across the dining room. Seconds later the back door slammed and the footsteps drummed on the porch and down the back steps.

At first Dena remained fixed on the stairway. As soon as she could move, she ran to the dining-room window that overlooked the back yard. No one was in sight. The smoothly clipped lawn lay empty save for the flower beds and trees and the row of bushes that enclosed it on three sides. Beyond were the spruce woods.

Dena went into the kitchen and made sure the back door was locked. Then she put a chair against it.

She had started toward the study to phone the constable when the bell on the front door rang. The sound threw her into a panic. Perhaps the man had circled around the house and was trying a new strategy.

But it could be her mother coming home early, or a neighbor. *Oh, Mom!* she thought. *I hope it's you. I need you.* Slowly Dena went into the living room. Again the bell rang.

Through the glass in the top of the door she could see a familiar face. To her relief the person on the porch was Guy O'Neill.

Dena flung the door open and seized Guy's hand as if he were an old friend.

"Hey!" he exclaimed. "I didn't think you'd be that glad to see me!"

"Right now I'd be glad to see anyone," she admitted honestly. "Someone just broke into our house. He just this minute ran out the back door." She found that she was shaking.

Guy brushed past her. "Which way did he go?"

"I don't know."

Guy raced to the kitchen and burst into laughter when he saw the barricaded door.

"Well," said Dena defensively, "I didn't want him to come back in." She unlocked the door and Guy rushed onto the porch with Dena close behind.

He looked in all directions and then leaped down the steps at one bound. "I'll try to find him." He paused. "What did he look like?"

"I didn't see him. But he sounded heavy." Dena ran down the steps. "Don't go. He might have a gun.

And if he's in the woods he could shoot you before you even saw him."

"I'll be careful."

"If you go I'm going with you."

"No you're not!"

Dena lifted her chin and looked at him with determination in her brown eyes. "You can't stop me."

"Now, look, Dena." Guy sounded annoyed. Then suddenly he laughed. "What a crazy chick! All right, you win this time."

"I'm going to call the constable." Dena ran up the steps.

"He'd be out on his boat now. Why not wait and let Paul report it? For all you know he may have sent a fellow here to get something for him and you scared him off."

"No way!" said Dena. "He picked the lock to get in. I heard him poking at it. And he ran when he heard me."

"Yeah?" Guy looked up at her with sympathy in his eyes. "I bet you were scared."

"My knees still feel shaky."

"You haven't eaten yet, have you?" Guy came up the steps to the porch. "That's what I came over for. My aunt and uncle said I could invite you to lunch. Uncle Earl said it was too bad you were going to eat alone the first day you came back."

"How did you know I'd be alone?"

"Aunt Irene said your mother's in Gullport and I

thought Paul must be hauling traps."

"Oh. Clever." I'm getting too suspicious, thought Dena. She considered Guy's invitation. She had refused to go home with Gramp and Barney. But the situation was different now. She no longer felt like staying in the empty house.

"Yes, thanks. I'm not hungry any more, but I'd like to go. Wait'll I lock the house. Not that it'll do any good. That—visitor—was good at picking locks." She hesitated. "Maybe I ought to stay here in case he comes back."

Guy reassured her. "He won't come back. Probably he's still running."

Dena giggled. "He can't be as scared as I was. Come on. Let's see if he took anything. He was in the study."

Probably whenever Mom and Paul were on the island both of them used the study for marking papers, making lesson plans, writing letters, and paying bills the way they used the big desk in the living room at the apartment.

At spring vacation Dena had noticed the desk at the apartment was no longer piled with papers and books as it had been when her mother had used it alone. Paul must be the neat type. Was that why he had moved to the tower room? So he could have a place to himself and not have Mom's stuff in his way?

Now as she and Guy came into the study she could see that all of the desk drawers were open. Papers were scattered on the floor and the desk chair was overturned. That explained the crash she had heard.

Guy bent to pick up the chair.

"Wait!" cried Dena. "Leave everything the way it is. Don't you ever watch detective stories on TV? When there's a break-in you're supposed to leave things alone so the police can figure out what the thief was looking for and they can get his fingerprints."

Guy laughed. "OK, Perry Mason. Let's go home to lunch. The Cat's waiting outside."

"The Cat?"

"The golf cart, Dopey!"

"Oh! Wait'll I get my shoes."

As she and Guy rode toward his home he said, "Better not tell Aunt Irene about your burglar. She's already shook up about living out here on the island. She's used to having neighbors nearby. Uncle Earl keeps telling her she's safer here than in the city, but she doesn't believe it. She's not too keen on island life, anyway."

"I'll be careful," agreed Dena. "Yesterday I would've said your uncle's right. Now I'm not so sure." She shuddered. "What a weird feeling to hear that fellow trying to get the door open."

Guy encouraged her. "You're doing great. Some girls would be screaming."

Dena began to feel less shaky. The ride in the golf cart was fun and she was comforted by Guy's kindness. How lucky for her he had come along at just the right time.

The Nelson house that Guy's uncle had bought was one of the largest on the island. Like most of the houses on Sebastian, it was painted white and was surrounded by a smooth lawn. A large blond man whom Guy identified as Frank was cutting the grass with a power mower, going carefully around the trees, many of which had been twisted and broken by the winter storms that often hit the island.

As the Cat rolled down the long driveway, two huge German shepherd dogs ran out to greet them. Guy stopped the cart and gravely introduced them to Dena.

He held her hand while he stroked the dogs. "Dena's our friend," he said. "You pet them," he told her. "They're good watchdogs, but they won't hurt you now that they know you're my friend."

Before they reached the house, Mr. Kaufman came down the driveway in a little Audi. He stopped and said in his courtly way, "I'm sorry to miss lunching with you, Dena, but I have to make a quick trip to the mainland."

Mrs. Kaufman had set a table on the patio on the east side of the house, overlooking the ocean. The chicken salad and frosty lemonade looked tempting. This promised to be a lot better than a peanut-butter sandwich.

"It's wonderful to have company for lunch!" said Mrs. Kaufman.

Even without being told, Dena would have known that this woman and Guy were blood relatives. Irene Kaufman was beautiful, with dark hair like Guy's, which she wore long and pulled smoothly back into a bun. Her blue eyes were like his, too, though hers had an anxious expression instead of the twinkle that made his so alive.

While she greeted Dena, the woman's worried glance took in the graveled driveway down which her husband had disappeared. A moment later she turned quickly toward the sound of the lawn mower still being operated by the blond man whom Guy had called Frank.

Still watching Frank, Mrs. Kaufman led Dena to the table. "I'm sorry your mother isn't home today, but it's a break for us, isn't it, Guy?"

"It sure is!" said Guy with enthusiasm. He pushed in his aunt's chair.

The food was even better than it looked. A husky young serving man named Walter passed hot rolls and kept the lemonade glasses full. Dena was fascinated by the way he walked. In spite of his size, he moved with the balanced grace of a dancer.

Mrs. Kaufman ate little of the delicious food. "I'm so glad to talk to someone new," she said. Her eyes and hands were constantly moving. "This past winter was the longest of my life. I felt so lonely. Guy was away at school and Earl was busy. He flies to Boston or New York or someplace every few days."

Guy explained. "Uncle Earl is president of a chain of restaurants. He does a lot of his business by phone but he says sometimes he has to make it on the scene."

Mrs. Kaufman's eyes had stopped traveling and now were staring fixedly toward the far end of the lawn. Dena followed the direction of her gaze. What was the big attraction? Was Mrs. Kaufman upset because Frank had stopped the lawn mower? Or was she concerned about the tall, thin young man with stooped shoulders with whom Frank was talking?

Guy said, "That fellow with Frank is Max Collier, Paul's helper. Probably you haven't seen him before, Dena. He lives over there." He pointed to a yellow house just visible to the south.

"My best friend used to live there," said Dena. "Maryann Kosac. We did everything together. Does Max live alone in the house, or does he have a family?"

"He's alone," said Guy. "Frank and Walter are single, too. They live in this house."

These three young men, Frank, Walter, and Max, all had moved to the island since last summer. It seemed strange. Life on the island must be dull for them. Had they come because they had jobs here? wondered Dena. Max helped on Paul's lobster boat and the other two apparently worked for Kaufman.

Max walked away toward the yellow house and Frank began to cut the fringe of grass around the

54

trees and flower beds with a pair of grass shears.

The conversation at the luncheon table faltered and died. Mrs. Kaufman's entire attention was on Frank, who was working his way closer and closer to the house. Soon he was trimming at the edge of the patio. His head, covered with tight, blond curls, bobbed above the hedge like an enormous yellow dandelion.

Mrs. Kaufman's hands were clenched on the edge of the table. "Frank, for heaven's sake, go eat your lunch!" she burst out. "Ask Walter to fix you a plate."

Frank said, "Great idea, Mrs. Kaufman," and lumbered away like a big, amiable bear.

Why was Guy's aunt so uptight about him? He looked nice enough and was doing a good job on the lawn. Yet, Dena could feel Irene Kaufman's tension like electricity in the air.

Dena tried to get the conversation started.

"Do you like to read or sew?" she asked. "My mother sews a lot when she isn't teaching."

"Yes, I like to read, but I find it hard to keep a supply of books on hand without a library nearby. As to sewing, I'd rather buy my clothes."

Mrs. Kaufman pushed aside her almost untouched plate. "Out here I can't even go shopping! There aren't any stores except for the one by the harbor and they never have anything I want." She sipped her lemonade. "Maybe I wouldn't mind if I were only here in the summer, like your mother."

"We used to live here all year when my father was alive," Dena told her. "But Mother's used to island life. She was born here."

Mrs. Kaufman sighed. "I'm afraid I'll never make a good island woman." She looked at Dena with big, sad eyes. "What's worse, Earl says he loves this quiet life and wants to retire here."

Suddenly she straightened up and gave a little laugh. "That's enough of my story." She passed the basket of rolls to Dena. "Do have another. They're a new recipe."

"They're wonderful. Everything is!" Dena said with honest enthusiasm. She was happy to see that her hostess appeared less worried.

Mrs. Kaufman put her hand briefly on Dena's. The sun dazzled on a huge diamond in her ring. "My dear, I have the feeling that everything in life is just wonderful for you."

Dena thought of her stepfather and her bouts with homesickness during the past year. "I have my moments," she said.

"She's human, you know, Aunt Irene." Guy looked at Dena with an intent expression in his eyes that made her feel as if he were seeing deep inside her mind. And that he liked what he saw.

Dena's cheeks burned.

"Of course. You're right, Guy," said his aunt. "I get to looking on the dark side too much. I should be thankful to be on this beautiful island. If only I could feel—safe."

"You worry too much about being safe!" Guy's tone was sharp. He pushed back from the table. "Come on, Dena. We'd better head for the airstrip."

Safe! Was it just island loneliness that made Mrs. Kaufman so nervous? Or had something happened to disturb her? Had someone broken into her house, also?

Dena felt again her terror at the sound of strange footsteps running across the dining-room floor. She wondered if she, herself, would ever again feel safe.

7

The *Martha* Is Gone

The airstrip was a mere track across the flat, grassy field at the southern end of the island.

When Dena and Guy arrived, Gramp and Barney were already there.

"Did you come to meet Mother?" asked Dena.

Gramp said grimly, "Nothing so pleasant. My boat has disappeared."

"How could it?" demanded Dena.

"I'd like to know." Gramp raised his arms and let them drop in a gesture of defeat. "You heard Sam tell me the *Martha* wasn't at the wharf at six this morning?"

Dena nodded.

"My guess is someone took her during the night. Of course I can't say for sure. I can't see the bay from the house." Gramp waved across the field to the east where his big log house stood on a rise. Behind it was a woodland and out of sight beyond that was East Bay. "I didn't go near the bay this morning. I headed straight for West Harbor to meet Barney."

Guy asked, "Did you look for her?"

"I did. Sam loaned me his boat so I could scout around, but not a sign of old *Martha*. Now I hope we can go up in the plane and get a wider view."

"Hi, there!" someone called.

Dena saw her stepfather coming across the field from the east.

"I was afraid I'd be late," he said as he joined them.

"You cut it kinda fine." Guy was looking at the sky where a small plane was circling for a landing.

The five people on the ground fell silent, watching the plane drop toward the island and finally touch down on the grassy airstrip.

As soon as it came to a halt Dena ran forward. Janet Roth, the only passenger, jumped lightly to the ground and held out her arms.

She's still my mother, even if she is married to Paul and is Mrs. Roth now, thought Dena as they embraced. She longed to ask about the tower room, but this wasn't the time.

They walked hand in hand back to the waiting group.

"Janet, my love, you and Dena look like sisters," Paul remarked.

It's true, thought Dena. Her mother was as slim as a girl and she looked great with her dark blond hair straight except for that little flip just above her shoulders.

After hasty explanations, Gramp and Barney per-

59

suaded the pilot to take them up to search for the *Martha*.

"What a shame!" said Dena's mother. "I can't imagine anyone being mean enough to take Gramp's boat."

"That's not the only weird thing that's happened around here," said Dena.

While they drove back to the house, she told about the break-in. She and Guy were in the back seat so she couldn't see Paul's expression. But her mother turned around, her face suddenly pale.

"Oh, Dena! And you were alone in the house when he came!"

Dena tried to reassure her. "He wasn't interested in me. He was poking around in the study."

Guy came into the house with them. "I want to see the look on your face when you see your desk," he said to Paul.

Dena waved dramatically toward the open door of the study. "The scene of the crime!"

Mrs. Roth exclaimed, "Oh, dear! What was he looking for?"

Paul strolled into the room and righted the chair. After a quick glance around, he began to gather the papers from the floor, piling them on the desk. Dena had expected he would be more upset. He didn't even act surprised.

"We didn't touch anything," said Dena. "I thought we ought to leave it the way we found it for the police."

Paul looked up from where he was kneeling. "The police officer on Sebastian Island is not Sherlock Holmes, my dear Miss Watson. Our lobsterman-constable has never had to cope with anything worse than a window broken by some kid with a baseball. So we'll have to do our own detective work."

Guy brought in the groceries from the station wagon.

"I'll be going now," he said. "See you tomorrow, Dena? How about a picnic?"

"Sure," she agreed. "That'd be fun."

Guy lingered in the doorway. "Y'know what I wish?"

"No. What?"

"That you'd take me on a tour of the island. The only time I was here was for about a week this spring and it rained all the time. I didn't get around much."

"Sure. I'll hire out as your guide," said Dena. "I want to check on my favorite haunts, anyway." She was still amazed that Guy wanted to be with her. Well, what choice did he have? she asked herself. She was the only girl he knew on the island.

When Guy had gone, Dena's mother asked, "Did you get unpacked?"

Dena admitted, "I didn't even start."

"Let's go up now," her mother said. "I'll help you."

This was the chance Dena had wanted. As soon as they were alone she asked, "Mom, why did you let

Paul have my room? You know Dad gave it to me and I love it!"

Mrs. Roth sat down on the bed and looked up at Dena. "I hated to do it, but I hoped you'd understand. It means so much to Paul." She went on to tell only what Dena had already guessed, that Paul was writing a book on the birds of the island. "He thinks he can finish this summer."

Dena groaned. "It'll take him all summer?"

"I'm afraid so." Mrs. Roth opened Dena's suitcase. "Now tell me how you got home. And where did you stay last night?"

Her mother took the account of her night of freedom more calmly than Dena had dared hope.

"Only I don't see why you didn't think of sleeping at our apartment," she said. "Why, you could have bought a new jacket for the cost of that motel room."

When Dena and her mother came downstairs, Paul was on the phone. Dena heard part of the one-sided conversation.

"You did? . . . Great!" Paul whistled softly. "That far out! . . . Sure. Be glad to. . . . I'll be at the dock soon as I can get there. About fifteen minutes."

Paul hung up the phone and leaped to his feet in the quick, springy way he had. Seeing Dena in the dining room, he explained, "Gramp's located his boat, miles to the east. Wants me to take him out to get her."

"That's swell." Dena thought wistfully of the fun

of going into the Atlantic where the waves would be big enough to lift the lobster boat like a toy. But Paul would never take her.

She was amazed to hear him say, "Want to go along?"

"Do I!" Dena wheeled around and ran to the kitchen closet to get her oilskins and boots.

"We may be late for dinner," Paul told his wife. "But don't worry. I'll take good care of Dena—and me."

Dena smiled to herself. That was kind of Paul. He must know how scary Mom was about the ocean. She had been that way ever since Dad was drowned.

Dena followed her stepfather out the back door and into the spruce woods. Paul was like two people. He must have a split personality. Sometimes he was great, like now, but why had he acted so funny this morning? Why hadn't he wanted her to stay alone in the house?

An idea came into her mind. An idea so strange she told herself to forget it, but it was there, all the same. Had Paul known someone was going to break into the house? Was that why he had tried to persuade her to leave?

8

The Gray Plastic Bags

Paul set a fast pace, even through the woods where roots curled upward ready to catch a careless toe.

In two or three minutes they came out into the flowery meadow above the beach. Here the air vibrated with the humming of bees that were visiting the red and white clover.

Paul took the path that cut diagonally across the meadow. Dena muttered to herself as thorns on the raspberry and wild rose bushes that overhung the path scratched her bare arms and caught at the oilskins she was carrying. However, she didn't slow down because she knew it was important to locate Gramp's boat as soon as possible. Already it was after three o'clock and, if they didn't reach it before dark, it might be lost forever.

It occurred to Dena that Gramp could have notified the Coast Guard. Why were lobstermen so doggone independent?

As they hurried south they passed Beachcomber Cove where Dena and Barney had often searched for treasure washed up by the tide. Beyond that, great tumbled rocks formed a peninsula that jutted far into the water before curving to the south. This arm of land acted as a breakwater for East Bay where Gramp and Paul kept their boats.

The large white lobster boat that now rode the swells in the bay was one Dena had never seen before.

Dena caught up with her stepfather. "Is *that* your boat?"

"That's the *Tenaj*. Isn't she a beauty?"

"I'll say!" She was more than a beauty. She was a bigger, better-equipped lobster boat than Dena usually saw off Sebastian Island. A boat like that would cost thousands of dollars. How could Paul afford her?

As if he were reading Dena's mind, her stepfather said, "I put my life's savings into that little boat, but she'll pay off."

Two dories bobbed beside the long wharf where Gramp and Barney were waiting. Gramp must like Paul. He had never before shared his wharf.

Paul rowed them out and fastened the dory to the mooring. He was the first to board the *Tenaj* and by the time the others were on the boat he was in the small cabin which gave shelter from the wind and spray on three sides but was open toward the stern. The motor roared to life and seconds later they were heading out of East Bay.

Tenaj, puzzled Dena. Where did Paul get a dizzy name like that for his boat? Then, as if a light had suddenly come on in her brain, she realized what it was. *Tenaj* was Janet spelled backward! Paul had named his boat for Mom.

Paul gave the wheel to Gramp. "You know where you saw your boat. You might as well take us there."

Gramp grinned like a pleased child. "I've been hoping to get my hands on this boat. Mind if I see what she'll do?"

"Sure. Give her the gun."

The *Tenaj* leaped forward like a duck about to take to the air.

Barney and Dena exchanged glances. "I'd get heck if I raced the *Martha* like that," said Barney. "Not that she would go this fast, anyway."

Dena zipped up her waterproof jacket and tied the drawstring on her hood. She sat down on a box and leaned against the rail.

"This is the life," she told Barney. The fine spray on her face, the sun and the wind, the motion of the boat, all made her feel the joy of being alive. "Want to sit down?" She moved over, but as she shifted her weight, the box on which she was sitting flipped up and she slid onto the deck.

Laughing, Barney hauled her to her feet. "What a nut you are!"

The box had fallen onto its side with the open bottom exposed.

66

Barney picked up something from the deck. "What's this?" He held out what appeared to be a handful of gray plastic.

"I dunno. Where'd you find it?"

"Must have been under the box." Barney turned the plastic over in his hands. "It's a bag. No, several." He laid the bags on the deck to examine them better.

Dena crouched beside him. The bags were of heavy plastic, about half the size of a garbage bag, and they seemed to be nested one inside the other.

"They've been cut open," Barney pointed out. "I wonder what was in them. Someone took a lot of trouble to make a package like this."

"So whatever was inside wouldn't get wet?" suggested Dena. She jumped up. "Let's ask Paul."

She seized the gray bags and took them to the open cabin where Paul was talking with Gramp.

Before she had time to say a word, Paul snatched the bags from her hands. "Where'd you get those?"

"On the deck!" she said, hurt by his tone. She pointed to the empty box. "They were under that."

Paul stuffed the bags into a cupboard under the foredeck. "Something Max picked up. Regular junk collector."

Dena stalked back to Barney. The joy had gone from the day.

"What'd he say?" Barney asked.

"He makes me so mad! He had no right to snap at me just because I asked a question."

"Cool it," said Barney. "What's the matter with you? You didn't used to be so quick on the trigger."

Dena leaned her elbows on the gunwale and kept her eyes on the waves fanning out in the wake of the boat. "Just be glad he isn't *your* stepfather." She took a deep breath. "He said—those bags are some junk Max picked up. I suppose Paul's mad at him for cluttering up the boat, but he doesn't have to take it out on me."

They had traveled due east for an hour when Gramp called out, "There she is!" He pointed to the south where a lobster boat wallowed in the waves. It was the *Martha*.

Paul took the wheel and steered close to the other boat.

"It's riding low," remarked Dena.

Barney agreed. "Must've shipped in some water."

"If you can get close enough Barney can hold onto her with the gaff hook and I'll climb aboard," said Gramp.

Twice Paul drew close only to circle away. The waves threatened to pound the two boats together. On the third try he sidled neatly up to the other vessel. Barney held the gaff hook firmly over the rail of the *Martha* while Gramp clambered aboard.

"I'll hold it while you get in," Dena told Barney.

"OK." He gave her the hook. "Hang on!"

Dena braced her feet against the rail and pulled as hard as she could. Barney placed his hands on the rail

68

and vaulted over. Just as he did, the *Martha* rose on a swell, and Barney landed with one foot over the rail of the *Martha* and the other dangling on the outside. If Gramp's boat dropped close to the *Tenaj*, Barney's leg could be crushed.

Quickly Dena shoved at the *Martha* with the gaff hook. This was no time to hold the boats together. At the same moment Gramp seized Barney and pulled him onto the deck.

The danger was over. Dena carried the gaff hook back to the cabin.

"That was close," said Paul. He had been watching over his shoulder while he remained at the wheel. Now he kept the *Tenaj* near the *Martha* but far enough away to avoid collision.

Gramp shouted, "We're taking in water. Stick around."

A few minutes later he appeared on the deck. "I've got the motor going, and the bilge pump's working OK. We'll be all right."

"Great," said Paul. "Anyway, we'll follow you for a while."

At first the *Martha* traveled slowly, but gradually she rose in the water and moved more briskly.

When Paul drew up beside the other boat, Gramp motioned him on.

Paul veered to the north. "Might as well haul a few traps while we're here," he told Dena.

"You have traps out this far?"

"Almost this far. That's why I need a boat like this. One the size of the *Martha* wouldn't be safe out here in rough weather."

Paul was calm and friendly again and Dena tried to forget her annoyance with him.

"Look there." Paul pointed to the north. "There's one of my markers. See? My colors are orange and blue. When I pull up to it, will you fish it in?"

Dena took the gaff hook and waited, squinting over the water. Near an island that was little more than a pile of rocks, she saw a buoy with broad orange and blue stripes.

"Is that yours?" she called.

"Right." Paul slowed down and pulled up abreast of the buoy. "Don't fall in."

Fall in! thought Dena scornfully. She had helped Gramp haul traps for years.

Reaching out, she hooked the gaff expertly under the rope that was fastened to the buoy and pulled the buoy toward the boat.

It gave her a feeling of satisfaction to hear Paul say, "I can see you're no amateur at this."

Dena leaned her elbows on the gunwale, watching while Paul operated the power winch. As many times as she had seen it done, she waited eagerly for the trap to emerge from the water, dripping and hung with seaweed.

"There she is!" said Paul. "Makes me think of Triton rising from the sea, blowing his wreathèd horn."

Dena stared at him. "Not me. Never heard that one. Makes me think of pirates and sunken treasure."

Paul opened the door in the top of the trap. "Here's treasure. Six of 'em."

One of the lobsters was undersize and another was a female, carrying eggs. Paul threw them overboard.

"Four good ones left," he commented. "Not bad."

"Do you have any bait on board?" asked Dena.

"Yes, in that barrel. I have some left from the last time I was out."

Dena started toward the barrel.

"Wait a minute, girl," Paul said. "I'll take care of the bait. No need for you to get smelly."

Dena said indignantly, "I can do it." She didn't like being babied.

Paul laughed and tossed her a pair of rubber gloves. "OK. Go to it."

When she had stuffed the small, knitted bait bags, Paul put them into the trap and shoved it overboard. The line played out, and again the orange-and-blue buoy marked the place where the trap was located.

Before he went back to the wheel, Paul jotted some figures in a notebook. "I keep a record of what I get in each trap," he explained. "Look here. I check the depth of the water on the fathometer and make a note of it along with the number of lobsters I get at that spot. That way I know where it's worthwhile putting down a trap."

It was after six when they neared the island. Even

71

from a distance Dena could see that the *Martha* was not in East Bay. What had happened?

Paul exclaimed, "Good night! Gramp isn't in yet!"

Dena knew he had the same fear as she, that the *Martha* had run into serious trouble.

9

The Man on the Cliff

"We'll go over and sell our lobsters," said Paul.
"Maybe someone at West Harbor will know where
Gramp has gone."

He steered around the southern end of the island
and up the west shore. Even before they rounded the
breakwater, Dena saw Gramp's boat.

"Look!" She pointed to where it was propped up
on shore. "There's the *Martha!*"

"You're right." Paul swung the *Tenaj* into harbor
and pulled up beside the lobster car that was floating
there. "At least we know they made it safely to shore.
Maybe Gramp thought he'd better have her checked
over."

To Dena, the lobster car had always looked like a
raft with a shed built on top of it. Actually, it was a
large raft, about twice the size of the living-room
floor.

She climbed onto the car and watched while Paul's
lobsters were weighed and dumped into an un-
derwater crate where they would stay until the man

on the lobster car sold them.

As soon as Paul was paid, he thrust the money into his pocket and said, "Let's get home fast and give Gramp a call."

But when they reached home, Gramp was in the kitchen, straddling a chair backward and talking to Mrs. Roth.

"Hey, we spotted the *Martha* at the harbor," said Paul. "What's the matter with her?"

Gramp was unsmiling. "She has a bad leak."

"What'd she do? Hit a rock?"

Barney came into the kitchen from the dining room. "Yeah," he said. "On the inside."

Paul frowned. "Come again?"

"That's right." Gramp turned around and sat on the chair in the usual way. "Looks like someone took an axe and tried to chop a hole in the bottom from the inside. Guess they got scared and quit before the hole was big enough. Or else we got there before the old girl had time to sink."

Paul leaned on the kitchen table. "Can it be fixed?"

"Oh, yes."

"Well, in the meantime, you can use the *Tenaj*," said Paul.

"Say, thanks!"

Gramp and Barney stayed for dinner and the talk centered around the strange happenings on the island.

Paul said, "I wonder if there's any connection between your boat being taken and our break-in.

74

Gramp, did you report the theft of the *Martha?*"

"Yep. I let the constable know right away. Told him about the buoys being missing and my dory set afloat, too."

"Oh, I didn't know about the dory," Paul said.

"Your helper, Max, found it and brought it back to me. Nice of him."

"But what's behind all of this?" Dena's mother asked. "Everything that happens to you seems to have something to do with lobstering. Does someone want to take over your business?"

Gramp slapped the table with the flat of his hand. "You've hit it on the head, Janet. But it isn't just my business they want, it's the whole kit and kaboodle."

Paul looked alarmed. "What do you mean?"

"I mean someone wants to buy my place, the land, the house, East Bay. The whole thing. And I'm not selling. That land's been in my family for two hundred years." Gramp's hands were shaking. "No big real estate operator is going to turn this island into a—a summer resort!"

"Take it easy, Gramp." Paul reached across the table to cover Gramp's hand with his own. "You don't have to sell if you don't want to. What makes you think someone wants to turn Sebastian Island into a resort?"

"Why else would some fellow in Bangor offer me a hundred thousand dollars for part of an island in the middle of nowhere? He isn't going to find any gold or oil out here."

"Wow! A hundred thousand!" said Barney. "You didn't tell me it was that much."

Gramp glared at his grandson. "I wouldn't sell for a million. I've never even seen the fellow and I don't know if he's ever been to the island, but he keeps writing me letters and calling me on the telephone, trying to get me to sell."

Mrs. Roth said gently, "And you think he's behind all the trouble you've had lately. He's trying to force you off the island."

"That's it in a nutshell." Gramp wiped his perspiring face with his handkerchief. "Now you know."

"Why didn't you tell us sooner?" asked Paul. "Maybe we can help."

"I didn't tell because a lot of my friends around here would think I'm crazy to turn down money like that. Well, let 'em laugh at me. Sebastian Island and lobstering, they're my life."

Paul leaned back and ran his fingers through his thick red hair. "The first thing to do is stop whoever's tormenting you. Why don't you start with the constable? I mean, level with him. Tell him the whole bit. Ask him to try to get some help from the mainland."

Gramp lifted his head. A faint look of hope came into his eyes. "What about the fellow in Bangor?"

"We can't prove yet that he's behind your problems here on the island," said Paul. "But the next time he

calls, don't argue with him. Politely tell him you're
not going to sell, and hang up."

Gramp sighed deeply. "I'll try it. I'll try anything."
He got to his feet. "I better go feed my dog. Then I'll
call on the constable."

"I'll feed Hector!" offered Barney.

"Fine," said Gramp. "I'll take you up on that."

"Want to go along, Dena?" asked Barney.

She stood up. "Let's go."

Hector was lying in the late sun near the back door
of Gramp's log house. He jumped up awkwardly and
ran to greet them. When Dena crouched down, he
put his forepaws on her knee and kissed her chin.

"You're the best dog in the world," she told the basset
hound. "You never run away, do you? And you're so
loyal."

Hector seemed to know he was being praised. He
sat up in front of Dena and solemnly held out his paw
to shake hands. His sad brown eyes seemed to look
deep into hers.

While Barney unlocked the door and went in to get
the dog's dinner, Dena stayed outside to play with
Hector. She threw a stick and he retrieved it so
eagerly he almost tripped over his ears.

But when Barney appeared with his dinner, Hector
was through playing.

Dena watched him wolf down his food. "Poor fellow, he's sure hungry."

"I could feed him every hour and he'd still act

starved," said Barney. "He just likes to eat, I guess."

"Yeah," said Dena. "He isn't thin."

Barney set a dish of fresh water beside the doghouse. "Hector earns every bite he eats. Gramp says he barked at night several times lately and in the morning there'd be footprints. Too bad he can't patrol the bay, too."

Dena and Barney walked back toward her home, following the path above the shore.

"When we came over on the *Henrietta* you said Gramp had an idea who was bothering him," said Dena. "That's his idea, then, that the man in Bangor is trying to make it miserable for him so he'll be willing to sell?"

"That's about it."

"But you said Gramp wouldn't put it in a letter for fear it would be opened before it ever left the island. That sounds as if he has enemies on Sebastian."

Barney explained. "He thinks the man in Bangor has hired someone to bother him. And the fellow must be on the island or he couldn't come around at night and all that."

"Do you think Gramp will ever sell?" asked Dena.

"No way! When Gram died my dad tried to get Gramp to come live with us and he said he'd never leave Sebastian. If it were me, I'd take the hundred thou and buy me another island, maybe in the South Pacific."

"You would!" said Dena, laughing. She went back

to Gramp's problem. "It's so lonely for him here when you go home."

Barney grinned. "There's a nice widow over near the harbor who asks him for dinner once in a while. I think he's getting interested. He was telling me about her. He said she'd never take the place of Gram, but she's good company and she's a great cook."

"Oh, good." Dena felt better about Gramp's future. "Now if we can find out who's taking his boats . . ."

"We? You're in this, too?"

"Of course."

Barney picked up a stone and sent it sailing far across the sand and into the water. "I'm sure glad you're here, Dena. Makes a lot of difference having someone to talk things over with."

"Same here." If she were in trouble she knew Barney would be the first to help. He was a real friend. An old friend. Almost the same as a brother.

10

The Picnic

During the night, fog took possession of the island. When Dena looked out of the window in the morning the house seemed to be wrapped in cotton candy.

She wondered how Gramp and Barney were this morning. Then she thought of her picnic with Guy. This fog would ruin it. She wanted to show him around the island and what could he see today?

She was surprised how disappointed she was. She had known Guy for only a day, but already he was important to her.

And Guy's Aunt Irene would be lonelier than ever on a day like this. And more afraid. She'd be imagining people hiding in the fog.

She had said she ran out of books to read. Dena sank to her knees before her bookshelves. It was a sure thing that Mrs. Kaufman would be long past Nancy Drew. She might like *The Hobbit* or *A Wrinkle in Time*, but the most likely book for her, Dena decided, was an old history of Sebastian Island. She laid it on top of her desk ready to deliver on her next trip to the Kaufman house.

Her mother and Paul were still at the breakfast table when Dena went downstairs. It was too foggy to haul lobsters.

"Even with radar I'd have trouble," Paul said. "And I don't have radar. So I get a holiday." He leaned back in his chair. "I like fog."

In spite of her disappointment about the picnic, Dena found herself agreeing with him. There was something mysterious about the island when it was fog shrouded. She liked the eerie sound of the bell buoy and the hoot of the foghorn.

"Mom," she said. "Guy's aunt is awfully lonesome. I guess she doesn't have any friends on the island. Do you suppose you could invite her over some day?"

Her mother looked at her with warm approval. "That's thoughtful of you, dear. I certainly will. I'll call her today."

Dena was eating breakfast when Gramp Sebastian phoned.

Paul talked with him and came back to the kitchen to report.

"Gramp says they had a prowler last night."

"Did he get in?" his wife asked anxiously.

"He went into the shed that's attached to the rear of the house. It's where Gramp keeps his tools."

Dena asked, "Did they see him?"

"No. Hector barked up a storm and chased him away. Good thing Gramp has that dog."

The next phone call was for Dena. To her delight it was Guy.

"How about if I pick you up at ten o'clock?" he asked.

"But the fog?"

"It's lifting. Take a look."

Dena glanced toward the window. "You're right! I can see the trees. Great! I'll pack a lunch."

When Dena returned to the kitchen with news of her picnic, her mother looked anxious. "There are such strange things happening . . ." she began.

To Dena's joy, Paul cut in. "She'll be all right with Guy. Don't worry about it."

Dena started the tour of the island with the tide pools on the western shore where long rock shelves reached into the water.

Feeling like a schoolteacher, she asked, "You know what tide pools are, don't you?"

"I guess so. Places where some water stays even when the tide goes out. I never really looked at one, if that's what you're getting at."

Dena crouched beside a shallow pool about two feet in diameter. "They come in all colors. This one's mostly orange and green."

Guy set down the lunch bag and knelt beside her. "Cool. But what's to see?"

"You have to look a while." She pointed. "There's a sea urchin. That little round pincushion. It eats seaweed."

"It doesn't look as if it would eat. Looks like a plant." Guy stirred the water with his finger and the waves sent a snail shell scurrying across the pool.

Dena made a quick grab for the shell and brought it out dripping. "Look who's living in this snail shell." She held it up for Guy to see. Tiny legs and pincers hung out of the opening.

"That's no snail!"

"It's a hermit crab. He moves into empty shells because he doesn't have a shell of his own. It's about time for this one to move out. He's getting too big for his home." She gently dropped the hermit crab back into the water.

Guy leaned closer to the little pool. "I never knew there was so much to see in one of these puddles. Look at that red flower."

"That's a sea anemone and it isn't really a flower. It's a killer. If anything it can eat touches its petals it sends out stingers and then it stuffs the paralyzed critter into its mouth. That hole in the middle of the flower is its mouth."

"Good night! Life's more dangerous in there than out here in the world!"

They began to circle north around the island, stopping at Kaufmans' to leave the book for Guy's aunt.

By noon they were a quarter of the way down the eastern shore near the old stone schoolhouse where Dena had attended first and second grade.

They spread their lunch on a flat rock in the meadow above the shore. As they ate they could watch the tide climbing higher and higher on the sand beach below them.

Guy leaned on one elbow, eating a tuna-fish sandwich. "I never want to live anyplace else," he said contentedly.

That reminded Dena of Gramp. He didn't want to leave the island, either. She wanted to tell Guy about Gramp's problems, but she decided not to. Gramp didn't seem to want everyone to know.

Dena peeled a tangerine onto a piece of waxed paper. "Wish we could live here all the time the way we did before my father was killed."

"What happened to him?"

"He was out hauling lobster and got caught in a bad storm. He must have been washed overboard." Even now she could remember the darkness of those days when they had waited and hoped. "We never will know for sure what happened."

Guy's expressive face saddened. "I'm sorry. And I know how you felt because I lost my father and mother in a plane crash—three years ago."

"Oh, Guy! Both of them at once." Tears of sympathy made a blur of the grass and daisies beside the rock table.

Guy looked out at the ocean, stern faced. "I was lucky to have Aunt Irene. She and Mom were sisters. She's done everything she could."

84

"And your uncle?" asked Dena.

"He's—away a lot."

That didn't answer my question, thought Dena, but she let it drop. He'd tell her more when he was ready.

When they had finished their lunch they ran up a path through the meadow toward the old schoolhouse.

Finally Dena slowed down to catch her breath. She looked back toward the ocean.

"How about those paths?" She motioned toward the trails where the grass had been flattened or worn away. They made a pattern like the spokes of a wheel with the schoolhouse as the hub.

"There's one from the north—could be from your house," she said. "And another from down that way. Might be from our house or Max Collier's. Why would people beat a path to an empty school? It hasn't been used since they built the new school when I was in second grade."

Guy turned to view the paths. "I think Max and some of his friends come here. I just thought of it now. I was at Max's house one night during spring vacation—I used to hang around with him some—and he said, 'You'll have to leave because I'm going out.' I said, 'Where can you go around here?' And he laughed and said he was going to school."

What could Max and his friends do at the schoolhouse? wondered Dena. Play cards and drink beer?

85

They had reached the front steps of the building. "Let's go in," said Dena. "I'd like to see what my old school looks like now."

"Why not?"

Dena ran up the steps and pressed the latch with her thumb. "It's locked." She stepped back, disappointed. Was every place on the island locked nowadays?

Guy ran his hand across the solid wooden door. "With a little work this would make a good house. I'd like to live here." He turned around and motioned toward the ocean. "Cut down two or three trees and you'd have a great view. Let's see if the back door is open."

That, too, was locked. Dena was ready to give up, but Guy wasn't satisfied. He circled the building, testing the cellar windows until he found one that was not fastened. When he pushed on it, it swung inward.

"Want to go in?"

A spider hurried on a slender thread across the opening.

Dena shuddered. "Ugh! Spiders! No, thanks. You go ahead."

Guy pulled the window shut again. "I can wait. Maybe Max has a key. I'll ask him sometime." He put his hand on the weathered stone. "I might like to buy this place if the price isn't too high."

"Ha!" said Dena. "How could you buy it?"

"With money, like anyone else. My father and mother left me some." As if to prove his point he added, "I bought myself a boat, a twenty-footer with room for five or six people. It can't compare with my uncle's cruiser, but it suits me. Even came with a good two-way radio."

Dena laughed. "You're out of my league. I couldn't buy a rowboat."

Suddenly Guy lost his confident air. "I can't throw it around. I don't have all that much. If I want to put myself through college—and I do—I have to hang on to what I have." He admitted, "I got a real buy on the boat, secondhand."

When they reached Gramp's log house, Gramp and Barney were not at home. Dena guessed they were out in Paul's boat hauling lobster traps, so she showed Guy the fresh-water pond south of the house where hundreds of ducks were swimming.

"Gramp feeds them when wild food's scarce," she said. "So no wonder his place is so popular."

From the pond they followed a stream to little Tom Thumb Bay at the end of the island.

They ended the tour with ice cream cones at the store. Several of her friends were there, and she introduced them to Guy. For half an hour they all sat on the grassy hill above the harbor and talked. Dena was glad to see how well Guy fitted in with the islanders.

As they walked down the road to Dena's house

they had little to say, but it was an easy silence.

When they reached her home Guy said, "This was a super day. I'll remember it always."

"Me, too," said Dena. Guy, like Barney, was a friend. But he didn't seem like a brother.

He gave her a smile that made her forget how weary she was. "I'll call you tomorrow," he promised.

11

Hector Disappears

A storm broke during the night.

Dena awakened at three in the morning when wind-driven rain pelted her face and bare arms.

When she leaped out of bed to close the windows she had left wide open the night before, her bare feet squished across the wet carpet.

For fifteen minutes she sopped up water with bath towels while the rain beat against the windows in gusts that seemed ready to break the glass. Yet, when she tumbled into bed, she soon fell asleep, thinking about Guy.

At seven-thirty the sky was a dull gray and the rain was still falling. The wind was, if anything, more furious than it had been during the night. Dena wished she were in the tower room so she could see the full beauty of the storm.

The lobstermen would have a day off, that was sure. Dena pulled on her robe and hurried downstairs, knowing that breakfast would be special today. As she had guessed, there were bacon, eggs, and coffeecake.

"You have to try harder on dark days," her mother had said more than once. Now she was teasing Paul, who was in the kitchen. "You're going to love it! I'm having a party. Mrs. Kaufman's coming, and Vi Hazlett and another island friend I think Guy's aunt might like."

Paul moaned and looked toward the streaming windows. "It's a terrible choice."

"Don't you *dare* go out today!" said his wife. "You'll have a marvelous time. You can go up to the tower and write without anyone to bother you. Dena and I will be busy all morning fixing the luncheon."

A knock sounded on the back door.

Paul jumped to answer it while Mrs. Roth murmured, "Who'd be out on a morning like this?"

Gramp came in and stood at the door, seemingly unaware of the streams of water that ran from his rain gear onto the clean kitchen floor.

"Have you seen anything of Hector?" he asked.

"No." Paul looked astonished. "Is he out in this rain?"

Mrs. Roth said, "Take his coat, Paul. Come on, Gramp. Have a cup of hot coffee."

Gramp looked toward the door. "I ought to keep going. I don't know where he is. I only hope he found cover some place."

"He's a smart dog," Paul said. "He knows enough to come in out of the rain. Let's have your coat. I'll hang it over the tub."

Gramp gave in. "That coffee does smell good. I forgot breakfast."

Dena poured him a cup and her mother put more bacon into the pan.

While Gramp ate, the story came out. He had gotten up in the night as soon as the storm started.

"Hector usually sleeps in his doghouse," Gramp said. "But when the weather's bad I always bring him in the house. Guess I'm soft, but I think it might rain in on him or something and I can't sleep for worrying about him."

Gramp sipped his coffee and gave Dena a grateful look. "My, that's good."

Dena was impatient. "What happened? Did you let him in?"

"He wasn't in the doghouse. I can't find him anyplace. I've combed the island, just about."

Paul asked, "Man, didn't you go back to bed at all?"

Gramp had his mouth full of coffeecake so he shook his head. When he could talk he said, "You know Hector. He never goes away. Something's happened to him, I know. No use going to bed. I couldn't sleep."

The phone rang and Dena ran to answer it, hoping it was news of Hector.

Barney's voice asked, "Hey, is Gramp over there? He isn't here and he didn't even start the fire."

Dena explained, and added, "Come on over."

Soon Barney joined the others at the breakfast table.

Gramp left while Barney was eating. "I can't give up," he said. "Hector may be lying some place, needing help."

Dena sat down at the table with Barney. "I'll go out with you for a while," she offered. "I can't stay long because I have to help Mom get a fancy lunch."

Again the phone rang. This time Paul answered. When he came back to the kitchen he looked cross, but he said lightly, "I'll escape the ladies' luncheon, after all."

"You're not going to haul!" cried Mrs. Roth.

"Max insists. And when you get a helper who is that gung ho, what can you do?"

His wife turned pale. "Don't let Max tell you what to do. It's crazy to go out today. Please, dear."

Dena knew that her mother was remembering that long-ago storm. How could Paul be so mean!

If she stayed, Dena knew she would explode and say something she shouldn't. She ran out of the kitchen and up the stairs to her room. There she stood at the window biting her knuckles to keep from shedding angry tears.

The wind was as wild as ever, but the rain had slackened enough so she could see the gray ocean heaving like a tortured monster.

A movement on shore caught her attention. Someone was walking along the cliff south of the spruce woods with his head bent into the wind. He was making slow headway. Why, it was Max! No one else on the island was as lean as that or had those stooping shoulders. But how could it be Max when not more than two minutes ago he had been talking on the phone to Paul?

There was only one answer to that. Paul had not been talking to Max. He had lied. It was not Max who had called.

What was Paul trying to hide?

Max continued along the cliff edge to the south. Even if he hadn't phoned, he must be planning to go out in the boat. At least he was headed in that direction.

Dena dressed quickly and ran downstairs. Paul had left and Barney was ready to go out and look for Hector.

Dena paused in the kitchen doorway. She wanted to declare, "Paul lied!" But when her mother turned around from the window, her face looked old with worry.

This was no time to announce her doubts of Paul. Mom already had enough problems on her mind.

Dena pulled on her boots and oilskins. "I'll be back in an hour," she promised.

The rain had returned, heavier than before.

As soon as she left the porch it thudded against her yellow oilskin hood and ran off the peak of the visor.

Barney turned his back into the wind. "Where'll we start?"

"How about going to Gramp's? Hector could've crawled under something to keep dry. Even if he was hurt he'd get home if he could."

Talking was difficult in the open, but as soon as they reached the spruce woods, it was as if they had entered a room.

"What d'you think happened to Hector?" asked Barney. He wiped at his face with a wet hand.

"I don't know. Gramp says he never wanders away." A dark suspicion hovered around the edge of Dena's thoughts. She wanted to ignore it, but it kept bothering her. "I wonder. I mean, I can't help wondering if someone took Hector away."

Barney ducked to avoid a branch that hung over the path. "How could they? He wouldn't go with any stranger. And if they shot him we'd have heard the gun. Gramp and I were home all evening."

Dena didn't argue the point. Like Barney, she wanted to believe Hector was safe, curled up in some sheltered place, sleeping out the storm.

When they reached East Bay, Paul's dory was leaping on its mooring, and his lobster boat was out of sight.

"How come Paul went out on a day like this?" asked Barney. "It'll be wild out where he hauls."

"He's crazy. Or he's up to something." Dena had to tell someone about Paul or burst. She and Barney turned inland. The wind was now at their backs and it was easier to talk.

"That phone call this morning," said Dena. "Paul said it was Max. Before that he wasn't going out to haul, but after he talked on the phone he said he was going out because Max was gung ho."

"Wouldn't think he'd let Max boss him around. It's Paul's boat."

"Yeah. And that's not the half of it," Dena said grimly. "Right away after the call when I went upstairs I saw Max on the cliff south of the spruces."

"So? I don't follow you."

"He hadn't had time to get there. Don't you see, Paul said it was Max on the phone, but it wasn't. Now, why would he lie about that?"

"I don't know." Barney walked with his head down. "There's an awful lot I don't know about what's going on."

When they reached Gramp's, they started their search with Hector's doghouse, bending low to peer into the dim place where he usually slept on a thick rug. The rain had not reached the inside of the doghouse, so Hector had not been driven out by the storm.

"Under the porches," suggested Dena. "We had a cat that was hit by a car and the first place she headed was under the porch."

They circled the house with no success. When they returned to the back yard, Dena said, "I'd better go

95

home. I promised Mom I'd help. I'll come out again as soon as I can get away."

"Thanks. You're a real pal." Barney spoke huskily. "Guess I'll go over to the pond. Maybe Hector decided to chase some ducks."

Dena started away. A short distance past the doghouse her foot rolled on something on the ground. She stopped and looked for the object. It hadn't felt like a stone or a stick.

In a moment she located it in a puddle. It was a hard plastic tube with a needle at one end. The needle was broken and the tube was empty.

She ran after Barney, screaming, "Wait! Look what I found!"

Barney came back and examined Dena's find. "It's a hypodermic needle!" He pulled out the plunger and held the tube up to look at it more closely. "So that's how they caught Hector."

"How?"

"They gave him a shot. Knocked him out." His face was furious. "Probably threw darts till they hit him. Or tossed him something to eat so he'd stand still. You know what a chow hound he is."

Tears mingled with the rain on Dena's cheeks. "He—might be unconscious someplace."

Barney looked again at the tube and broken needle. "Wonder why they left this lying around?"

"It was out of sight in a mud puddle," Dena told him. "I wouldn't have found it if I hadn't happened to step on it. I'm sure they didn't leave it on purpose."

"Well, I'll find Hector! And I'll find out who did it!" vowed Barney.

12

Strange Discovery
on the Beach

In spite of the storm, the three luncheon guests arrived on time.

"Nothing could keep me away," declared Mrs. Kaufman, smoothing her black hair. She was still nervous. Dena noticed how she jumped when someone dropped a coat hanger.

Dena was proud of the way her mother kept the conversation going on topics that would be of interest to Mrs. Kaufman as well as the two island women. No one could have suspected how worried she was about her husband.

The guests laughed and talked, clearly having a good time. By the end of the meal, Irene Kaufman was looking less haunted and fearful.

As soon as she had finished the dishes, Dena went out again to look for Hector. The rain had stopped and the sky was clearing. She wondered what Guy was doing. He hadn't phoned so far today.

This time she went north through the woods,

searching the ground for a freshly dug grave. But she found nothing.

She came out of the woods near the old schoolhouse and turned south toward home on the cliff path. Halfway there she met Max. He was carrying his lunch pail and a large duffel bag. It was the first time she had met him face to face, but there was no mistaking that thin figure and the bent shoulders.

Dena introduced herself and then exclaimed, "I'm glad you're back! Where's Paul?"

"Coming. He's cleaning up the boat." It was clear that Max didn't want to stop to talk. Even while he was answering, he edged past.

Dena was almost home when she saw Paul approaching. She waited for him on the cliff.

"Hi!" she called. "Was it bad out there?"

"The worst I've ever seen."

"Why did you go?"

Paul shrugged. "I asked myself that several times."

"Max didn't call you this morning," she said accusingly.

Paul met her eyes. "You're right. It was Frank on the phone. He had been talking to Max, and Max was in a hurry to get started, so Frank called me."

"Oh!" Dena's spirits rose. Now maybe I'll stop jumping to conclusions, she thought.

Paul said, "I'm glad you come right out and ask about things that puzzle you. I like you the way you are."

This surprised Dena. "Then why did you send me away to school?"

Paul laughed. "See? You don't beat around the bush. And neither will I. To begin with, I didn't send you away. Your mother and I talked it over and we both agreed we'd like you to go away to school to get a broader view of the world. Here on the island you don't meet many people. You have a good mind and it deserves to have a chance."

"I'll get enough broadening when I go to college."

"Are you sorry you had a year in boarding school?" asked Paul.

Dena tried to give an honest answer. She hadn't liked the idea of being sent away, but had she actually disliked the school? "I was homesick part of the time," she said, "but I made some good friends and I learned to ski. And I liked the teachers. No, I guess I'm not sorry I went."

"Good. That's what I hoped." He stopped in the path and looked seriously at Dena. "I had another reason for wanting you to go."

She wondered what was coming. "Go on," she urged.

"I wanted some time alone with your mother."

Dena stared at her stepfather, trying to understand. When you were as old as Mom and Paul, she hadn't thought it would matter if you were alone or not. She tried to put herself in Paul's place. Did he feel about Mom the way she felt about Guy? She liked to be alone with Guy, and she wasn't even in love with him. Not yet, anyway.

But if Paul and Mom wanted to be alone, where did that leave her? Out in the cold. Well, they'd have to put up with her this summer. In the fall she supposed she'd be going back to boarding school. Or would she? Paul had asked if she was sorry she'd had a year in boarding school. That didn't sound as if he meant her to go away again.

Well, she'd wait and see. She didn't want to live at home if Paul didn't want her there.

Late that afternoon Paul took his lobsters around to the lobster car. When he came back Dena and her mother had dinner ready.

"I stopped at Gramp's," Paul said. "He was sound asleep in his big chair, so Barney and I went outside to talk. Gramp didn't even know I was there, poor fellow. He combed the island for a trace of his dog."

"Didn't they find a sign of him?" asked Dena's mother.

"Not a clue, except for the hypodermic Dena and Barney found. It doesn't look good."

After dinner Dena decided to call Guy. He had said he would phone and she was sure he was the type who kept his word. Perhaps he had tried to reach her when she wasn't home. Or he might be ill.

She had the study to herself because Paul was in the tower.

Guy himself answered.

"How are you?" asked Dena.

"Fine."

"Well, I just wanted to make sure," she said. Guy wasn't helping her at all. "I've been out a lot of the time today and I thought I might have missed your call."

"No. I didn't phone."

"Well, then. I won't keep you."

"Uh. Yeah. See you around."

When Dena hung up she felt bewildered. The boy on the other end of the line was like a stranger, completely different from the warm and friendly Guy she knew. What had happened since they had parted at the door yesterday?

Restless and puzzled, she decided to go out again to search for Hector. That was one problem she could tackle. As to Guy, she would just have to wait and see.

She told her mother where she was going and went out the back door.

The air was fresh and cool after the storm. The wind tossed her hair and flattened her sweater against her body.

Hector had to be *someplace*. As she went through the spruce woods behind the house she could see the basset hound as clearly as if he stood before her, his sad, loving eyes fixed on her, his long ears dangling below his chin.

But when she came out of the dim woodland, the

image of the dog vanished.

First she'd go to Gramp's and find out if there was any place on the island where he and Barney had not searched. But when she reached East Bay, she saw Barney walking along the shore. Even at a distance she could tell by the slope of his shoulders that he was tired. She ran down the cliff to meet him.

"I swear we've gone over every inch of the island," he said. "So I've started on the beaches." He drew in a deep breath. "If they took him out to sea . . ."

"Come on," said Dena. "I'll go with you."

They followed the shore of East Bay north to the end of the sand beach. Then they climbed across the piled boulders that made up the peninsula.

Beyond the rocks lay Beachcomber Cove. Debris from the storm marked the high-tide line, and out beyond the sand flats the waves were still pounding with unusual force.

Dena picked up a starfish that looked dead, but when she turned it over she saw that the tiny tube feet were moving in and out.

"Look here!" Barney shouted. He was ankle deep in the water, holding up a dripping bag.

Dena set the starfish on the sand and ran to see Barney's discovery.

"That looks like the bags we found on Paul's boat!" she cried.

Barney set the bag on the sand. "Except this is whole. I don't see any breaks in the plastic. And it feels as if something's inside it."

Dena turned the bag over and pressed it between her hands. There was still air inside.

"I think there are other bags in this, just like we saw on the boat. And I can feel something like a small package. Let's find out what it is."

"Sure," agreed Barney. "We'd better take it home to look at it." He raised his head and scanned the cliff.

Dena followed the direction of his gaze. Were eyes watching them from behind a rock or bush? Or from Max's house?

Barney hurried to the shelter of the cliff. There he brushed the sand from the bag and stuffed it under his jacket.

Dena laughed at his suddenly bulging chest. "Who do you think you're kidding?"

Barney tried to flatten the bulge. "Maybe we won't meet anyone."

No one was on the cliff when they reached the top and they met no one on the way to Gramp's.

Gramp laid the bag on the kitchen table as if it were a patient on an operating table.

"The top is sealed," he noted. "It's absolutely air and water tight." He removed a pointed knife from the rack by the sink. "An incision is necessary." He made a neat cut in the gray plastic, and it fell open to disclose another gray bag. Again Gramp's knife made a long slit. Another bag. Another flash of the sharp knife and another bag.

Gramp checked with his big, capable hands. "We're getting close to the tumor. I don't want to cut into it."

Dena and Barney leaned over the table while Gramp worked more cautiously than before. The last bag fell open and there in the center of the nest of bags was a package, no more than six inches long, neatly sealed in plastic.

"What's your guess?" asked Gramp. "Diamonds? Rubies? Gold dust? Microfilm?" He picked up the small package and nicked a hole in one end. "Or something more expensive than any of them?"

He poured a small trickle of fine white powder into the palm of his hand. "What d'you think that is?"

"Heroin," said Dena.

Barney nodded. "That's my guess, too."

"Oh, you TV kids know too much." Gramp sniffed at the substance. "No smell, and heroin is odorless, so that checks. If it's heroin, it tastes bitter, but since I'm not one hundred per cent sure what this is, I'm not going to taste it." He brushed the powder from his hand into a saucer. "I'm betting on heroin, too. If we're guessing right, someone has figured out a great way to smuggle dope into the country, and he's making a fortune."

Gramp resealed the small package with tape. "Can you imagine the human misery this little bundle can lead to? All the kids whose lives can be ruined by it?"

Dena felt as if her mind were a crowded street where thoughts rushed up and down and crashed into each other. Had the bags on Paul's boat once contained a package of heroin? Was he a smuggler? Was there any connection between the disappearance of Hector and that little package of white stuff that looked like talcum powder?

Barney said, "Paul and Max went out this morning."

"Let's not leap to any conclusions," warned Gramp.

"I can't help it." Barney went to the window and stared out at the sky, now turning pink in the sunset. "The bags we found on Paul's boat were just like these."

"He could've found them floating." Gramp sighed. "I don't want to believe Paul is involved in anything like this. And we could be guessing wrong about this being heroin or horse or stuff or smack or whatever they're calling it now. It may be something innocent."

Dena said nothing, but a fear gnawed at her stomach. Was this why Paul and Max had gone out in such bad weather? To pick up gray plastic bags like this? Had this bag gotten away from them in the storm?

Gramp frowned at the packet he was holding. "The *Henrietta* comes tomorrow. I'll go to town and get this stuff analyzed. I'll take it straight to the police. No use going to our constable with it." He started toward his bedroom with the package. Suddenly he whirled around. "Did anyone see you pick up that bag?"

Barney looked shaken. "I—I don't think so. I didn't see anyone. But when I first found it I had a funny feeling, like someone was watching."

"Pull those curtains, Barney." Gramp paced nervously and at the same time he rolled the gray bags into a tight bundle. "I'd burn these, but they may be evidence. And where'll I hide the package?"

Dena helped to draw the flower-patterned curtains. The kitchen looked cozier than ever with the world shut out and the lamplight gleaming on the floor and the white-chinked log walls.

"We need Hector," said Barney sadly.

"If anyone saw you, they'll come here tonight, looking for this package," said Gramp. "If I had my boat I'd head for shore right now. I'd call the plane, but they can't land here at night. It's getting dark already." Gramp scanned the room. "Where'll I hide this stuff?"

"In the woodbox," suggested Dena.

Barney said, "I'll take it to bed with me."

Gramp shook his head. "Keep thinking."

"We could bury it," said Barney.

"They may be watching the house now."

Dena wandered around the room, looking for hiding places. She ran her hand along the mortar that filled the cracks between the logs. "Is any of this loose?"

Gramp's face lighted up. "Yes! Near the fireplace. I've been meaning to fix it." He poked at the mortar and a long strip came out in his hand. He peered between the logs. "Plenty of room for this packet."

"What about the bags?" asked Barney. "If they find the bags they'll know we have the package."

"Give them to me." Gramp held out his hand. "I think there's room for them, too. I can flatten them out."

A few minutes later the bags and package were between the logs and the strip of mortar was back in place.

"They might torture you to find out where it's hidden," said Dena.

"Could be," said Gramp. "But I don't plan to let them in. Barney, you and I will take turns sleeping tonight."

Dena was not satisfied. "Why don't you phone the constable?"

"Maybe I should, but word might get to the wrong people. I have an old gun. I'm not much of a shot, but I could scare away a prowler." He put his arm around Dena's shoulders. "It's time you were leaving. And don't worry about us."

Barney said, "I'll walk you home."

That night Dena pulled a chair close to her window and made herself comfortable for a long vigil.

Again she wished she had the tower room. She had decided to stay on guard all night, and if she saw a person walking to the south she would phone Gramp and Barney.

While she waited, she had plenty of time to think. She went over her short telephone conversation with Guy. He hadn't sounded natural. Did he feel awkward because he was in a room with someone who was listening? Or had she only imagined that he liked her and wanted to be friends?

Her thoughts wandered to Paul. Why did he really want the tower room? So he could watch for signals? He didn't seem to spend much time up there.

Anyway, it wasn't a signal that had sent him out today, but that message from Max. Max must be the one who had picked up the signal that a bag of heroin was being delivered.

That had been a surprise, hearing Gramp rattle off those street names for heroin. He was a wise one!

Where was Hector tonight? Wherever he was, she hoped he was not suffering.

Finally Dena fell asleep with her head on the window sill. Sometime in the night, without knowing it, she crawled into bed.

13

Round Trip to Gullport

It was nine-thirty when Dena awakened the next morning.

At once she thought of Gramp and Barney and the package they were guarding.

Paul would be out on his boat now, so she could phone Gramp and find out if anyone had come during the night.

She dressed hurriedly and ran downstairs, but to her dismay Paul was in his study. How could she ask Gramp about the heroin with a possible smuggler sitting beside the phone? On a fine day like this, Paul should be out in his boat or studying the birds.

He was still at his desk when Dena had downed orange juice, toast, and a glass of milk.

She had to make sure Gramp and Barney were safe. Of course she could go to see them, but by the time she walked there they might be on the way to catch the mailboat.

That was the answer!

Dena found her mother in the basement putting

clothes into the washing machine. "Want me to get the mail and go to the store?" she asked.

"I'll say I do. Get some fresh lettuce and vegetables. I'm glad you thought of it. The fresh things are sold so fast."

The dock and the roadside in front of the store were crowded with people who had come to meet the *Henrietta*.

Dena climbed the hill overlooking the harbor and tried to find Gramp's curly gray head or Barney's lionlike mane on the wharf. Neither was there.

Then she saw Guy. He was sauntering down the road toward the wharf, carrying the blue gym bag.

He must be going to town on the mailboat. Otherwise, why would he be carrying the blue bag? He was dressed for the boat trip, too, in a tan windbreaker. In spite of the crowd, Dena could follow him easily as he made his way to the end of the wharf. What made him so—noticeable? Was it because he was tall and good looking? Or because she liked him?

She tore her gaze away from Guy's dark head in time to see Gramp and Barney coming up the road from the south. Gramp was not carrying anything. What had he done with the packet?

Dena left her post on the hill and ran down the road.

Gramp and Barney were on the wharf by the time she caught up with them, and several men and women were within earshot.

"Any sign of Hector?" she panted. At least that was a safe question.

"Not a hair," said Gramp.

Barney gave Dena a knowing look. "It sure was quiet around our house last night."

Gramp patted himself on the stomach. "And Barney fixed us a good breakfast this morning. I think I'm getting fatter already."

Yes, there was a new bulge just above Gramp's belt. So that was where he was carrying the plastic-wrapped package.

A horn sounded behind them and Dena jumped aside to let a pickup truck drive past. The boat was in and already the cargo was piling up on the wharf. The tide was not as high today as on the morning when she had arrived, so the men on the deck of the *Henrietta* were handing the crates and bundles up to the men and boys who were kneeling on the wharf. She wondered where Guy was.

"Bon voyage," she said to Gramp and Barney.

"You don't have to say good-bye to me," said Barney. "Come on. I'll stake you to a bottle of pop. I have to wait for the mail."

"Hi!"

Dena recognized Guy's voice. She turned quickly and almost collided with him.

"Oh, hi!" Stupid me, she thought. Why can't I come up with a bright remark?

"You going to town?" he asked.

"No. Just came to get the mail and some groceries."

"I have to go to the dentist, but I'm coming back on the plane this afternoon."

"Oh, good."

He laughed. "What's so great about going to the dentist?"

"Good you're coming back today." Dena felt her face turn warm. That wasn't what she had meant at all. The word had just popped out because she was glad he was going to the dentist instead of delivering a bag of heroin to some unknown person—like the man in the Harbor Coffee Shop, for instance. She was glad, too, that he was his usual friendly self.

But as she and Barney went up the hill she began to feel less happy about Guy's mission in Gullport. If he were only going to the dentist and returning the same day, why did he need an overnight bag?

Barney was telling her something, but Dena had been so absorbed in her thoughts she had not understood him.

"What'd you say?" she asked. "I was in a fog."

"I said," he repeated slowly as if talking to a child, "Gramp is coming back on the plane after lunch. Why don't you come to the house and get a firsthand report on you-know-what?"

"OK. I will." She glanced around to see if anyone were near. For the moment they seemed to be alone, so she moved closer to Barney and asked quietly, "What happened last night?"

"Nothing."

"Nothing?"

"You heard me. We took turns watching, and no one came near the place. I came to the dock with Gramp in case someone tried to ambush him. Now he's on the boat and we can relax."

Dena was not so sure. "What about on the boat? If they—whoever they are—know he has the package with him they could push him overboard."

Barney stared at her with anger in his hazel eyes. "You have too much imagination!"

At first Dena was hurt by his anger. Then she realized he was cross because he was afraid she was right that Gramp was still in danger.

Dena was helping her mother make wild strawberry jam that afternoon when she heard the plane. She ran outside in time to see the little craft that acted as an air taxi for the people of Sebastian Island drop down toward the runway.

She hurried back into the hot kitchen where her mother was stirring a huge kettle of berries and sugar.

"Can you get along without me for a while?" asked Dena. "I'd like to go over to Gramp's for a few minutes."

"No way," said her mother. "I need you. Paul and I are invited to dinner at the Hazletts' at five-thirty. Even with your help I'll do well to finish in time to dress. I hope Paul gets in early."

Dena felt as if she might explode with impatience as she sterilized jelly glasses and helped to fill them. She and her mother were hard at work when Guy arrived.

"Can't stay," he said, standing in the middle of the kitchen. "Just thought I'd say hello on my way home."

"Have a sample," Dena's mother offered. "Clean out the pan and try it on a piece of bread."

Guy set down his gym bag and willingly scraped out the jam kettle.

"Was Gramp on the plane?" asked Dena.

"Yeah. We were the only passengers."

Dena felt better. At least Gramp was safe.

When Guy had gone, Dena said, "Go on, Mom. I'll wash the pans and clean up the kitchen." Now that Guy had come to see her, nothing seemed difficult.

"Would you? You're a dear. Oh, there's a casserole in the fridge for you. Will you put it in the oven?"

It was a large casserole, Dena discovered. Big enough for three, anyway. Large pieces of roast beef were nestled among chunks of carrots, onions, and lima beans. All were cloaked in a rich, brown gravy.

She ran up the stairs to ask, "Mom, OK if I take this casserole to Gramp's and eat with him and Barney?"

"I wish you would," said her mother. "And stay

there all evening. I don't like leaving you alone, the way things have been happening lately. And we may be late. We'll be playing bridge after dinner."

Dena, Gramp, and Barney ate early at the picnic table in front of the house. When they had cleared away the few dishes, Gramp sat in one of the rustic chairs he had made years before. He read the newspaper he had bought in Gullport while Dena and Barney played checkers at the picnic table.

Since the house was standing on a rise, they had a view of the airstrip and beyond it the sea that lay between Sebastian Island and the coast of Maine. The sun, still high in the west, made the air comfortably warm.

As Dena waited for Barney to figure out his next move, she thought about Hector. What could have happened to him? It didn't seem right not to have him lying beside Gramp's chair.

Gramp had brought back the word that it was heroin in the packet they had found, and the police in Gullport were turning the matter over to a special government agency that took care of drug problems. Dena tried to remember its name. The initials were DEA. D for Drug, but that was as far as she could go.

"Gramp," she said. "What does DEA stand for? I forget."

"Drug Enforcement Administration," he said patiently.

"Thank you." She repeated to herself, "Drug Enforcement Administration." She was willing to turn the mystery of the heroin package over to the DEA.

"It's your turn," said Barney.

Dena had just jumped two of his men when she stopped, checkers in hand, listening. Someone was coming. She could hear the swish of the grass. She turned in the direction of the footsteps.

Guy O'Neill was coming around the house toward them, carrying something in his arms, something that was wrapped in his tan jacket. He walked as if his burden was heavy.

Guy stopped in front of Gramp and laid the bundle in front of him.

"It's Hector," Guy said. "I found him in the water at Beachcomber Cove." His voice sounded harsh as he blurted out, "He's dead."

With that, Guy left as quickly as he had come. Only now he took the well-worn path toward West Harbor.

14

The Schoolhouse Cellar

At first no one spoke. Then Dena heard herself cry, "Oh, no!"

She felt the tears rain down her face, and when she looked at Barney and Gramp she saw that they, too, were crying.

Finally Gramp said in a choked voice, "You shouldn't look, but I have to." He knelt beside the jacket-wrapped bundle. "It was kind of Guy to bring him home. I'm afraid his jacket is ruined."

Barney asked, "Is there anything—to show what happened to him?"

"Not that I can see."

After a while Gramp went into the house and returned with a small blanket in which he wrapped the dog's body.

"I don't find a mark on him. There's no blood. That hypodermic needle you found may have taken his life."

Barney nodded. "I sort of gave up hope when we found that."

Gramp sank down into one of the lawn chairs. "Will you get the wheelbarrow and a shovel, Barney?"

"Sure, Gramp. But aren't you going to try to find out if he was poisoned?"

"Barney, that's a job for a toxicologist, and there isn't that kind of critter on the island. No, Hector's gone and nothing can bring him back."

Barney dug a hole on the small mound south of the house and the three who loved him most buried Hector.

Afterward Gramp said, "I'm going for a walk."

"Want me to go with you?" asked Barney.

"No, thanks. But if I'm not back by the time Dena's ready to go home, you see to it she gets there safe."

Tears came to Dena's eyes again as Gramp walked away. She knew how lonely he must be. He and Hector had lived together for a long time.

When Gramp was out of sight, Barney asked, "Did you get the feeling Guy knows more than he told us?"

"Well—I don't know. Maybe that he suspects something, but I'm sure he didn't—wouldn't—hurt Hector."

"Yeah, I know that." Barney went back to the picnic table where the checker game still lay. "Whose turn is it?"

They finished the game and Dena was the winner.

She began to stack the checkers in their box.

"Hey, what's the idea?" demanded Barney. "You quitting while you're ahead?"

"I don't want to play any more. What I want to know is whose body are we going to find next?"

Barney looked shocked. "You think they'd kill *us?*"

"They might if we're in the way. I'm glad Gramp went to the police with that heroin. And I hope the DEA gets over here fast." She folded the checkerboard. "I wonder if Guy could tell us more about what happened to Hector? Let's go ask him."

But Guy wasn't home when Dena and Barney arrived. His uncle met them at the door. "I'm sorry," he said. "Guy left about an hour and a half ago. He said he was going out in his boat. Is there anything I can do for you?"

"No, thanks," said Dena. "We just wanted to see Guy."

The sun was sinking low in the sky as she and Barney walked through the meadow. The trees sent long shadows across the grass turned gold by the sun's rays. Even the daisies and the Queen Anne's lace were gilded.

"I wonder why he was over by Beachcomber Cove?" pondered Barney.

"Maybe he was going to ask us to go with him," suggested Dena. "Then on the way he found Hector and didn't have the heart to ask us."

Barney said grumpily, "Did you ever think he

might've gotten the money for his boat by smuggling heroin? Paul, too. Look at that swell boat he has. Gramp has lobstered all his life and he couldn't afford a boat like that."

Dena fought against a feeling of despair. "Paul and Guy got their boats honestly. I know that. And I can't bear to believe they're mixed up in this. I like Guy. For a while I thought I hated Paul, but since I came home I've gotten to like him, too. Mom's going to feel terrible."

"Yeah. Paul seems OK. It sure is funny."

Dena walked with her head down, thinking deeply. "Maybe we ought to tell Paul and Max they're going to be caught and if they're guilty they'd better confess. The DEA is sure to arrest them. If they'd give themselves up, they might get off easier."

"But if they killed Hector, they deserve the worst."

"They *couldn't* have done that!" Dena was indignant.

"Someone did. I can't see Hector drowning himself. And I bet all of Gramp's troubles and the smuggling are connected."

Ahead of them was the old schoolhouse. Its windows glinted in the late sunlight.

"Guy told me he believes Max and some of his friends get together here," remarked Dena. "I thought they played cards and drank beer, but maybe they come here and plan things."

Barney said, "Like how to smuggle heroin and get

rid of Gramp's dog?"

"Yes. If Max is a smuggler, probably some of his friends are in with him."

"Don't forget Paul," Barney reminded her. "Maybe he comes here, too."

Dena looked up at the old building. "If Paul comes here for meetings there won't be one tonight because he and Mom have gone out to dinner." She glanced at Barney. "What d'you say we go in and look around. We might turn up some evidence."

"Can we get in?"

"The door's locked. But I know a cellar window that's open, and there's a trapdoor from the cellar to the schoolroom."

Barney hesitated. Then he said grimly, "I'll do anything to find out who killed Hector. Let's go."

"It isn't like breaking in," Dena reassured him. "This old building is owned by the town and it was abandoned."

He looked doubtful. "I don't think it's legal, but we're not going to do any damage, that's sure."

The loose window was still decorated with webs. Dena decided it was time to overcome her fear of spiders, but the thought of one crawling down her neck made her shudder. She solved the problem by brushing away the webs with a handful of grass.

The window swung inward on hinges at the top of the frame. While Barney held it open, she slid through and dropped onto the cement floor of the cellar. Barney followed her.

Almost blind in the dim light, Dena groped forward a few steps over the cracked and uneven cement. Gradually her eyes adjusted and she could see a broken desk in one corner and a bench against the wall near the open window. In the ceiling she located the square outline of the trapdoor toward the rear of the building. A ladder led up to the opening.

"It's just where I remembered!" she said happily. "When I was a kid I climbed down here once when we were playing hide and seek during recess. My friends came looking for me and the teacher didn't tell them where I was. I could hear everything they said."

Barney climbed the ladder and pushed the trapdoor open.

The schoolroom, with windows on two walls, was lighter than the cellar. In the center of the room was a long table surrounded by straight chairs. A few old school desks stood against the rear wall.

It did not look like a room that had been neglected for years. Even the table appeared to be dust free. Max and his friends must have cleaned the place.

"Look at the oil lamps!" said Barney.

"Sure. The electricity was cut off years ago."

Dena walked the length of the table, looking for scraps of paper or anything that might give her a clue as to what went on here. She saw no playing cards or empty beer bottles. The ashtrays were empty, but on the bottom of the single wastebasket she found a scrap of paper wadded into a ball.

She spread the paper flat on the table, smoothing out the creases with her hands. Someone had been doodling, that was all, drawing a picture of a bird. It was a bird with a curved beak like a hawk. Then she noticed something written under the sketch. The writing was faint, as if it had been erased.

Dena started toward the windows to get a better light on the paper, but halfway there she heard a sound outside. She stopped in the middle of the room, listening. Voices! And they were coming nearer.

She met Barney's eyes, and could tell by his startled expression that he, too, had heard. Stuffing the paper into her pocket, she ran to the trapdoor. Barney held it open and Dena dashed down the ladder.

Footsteps sounded at the entrance to the school and a key rattled in the lock. Barney lowered the trapdoor over his head with only seconds to spare.

Dena started toward the unlocked cellar window, but Barney seized her arm. She nodded in silent agreement. If she went outside someone might see her. Besides, if she and Barney stayed, they might hear something of interest.

She sat down on the bench near the open window and Barney joined her there.

Feet walked across the room above. Some stepped

lightly, but one pair had a heavy tread, reminding Dena of the footsteps of the man who had broken into her home the day she had arrived. There was little conversation.

Chairs scraped back and then a deep voice said, "Lock the door. Everyone's accounted for." Dena recognized the voice. It belonged to Earl Kaufman, and that was a surprise. He couldn't be one of Max's young friends. He was much too old and dignified for that.

"First order of business," said Kaufman. "Yesterday's shipment. Max."

So Max was there.

"Bad weather," said Max's voice. "But we managed."

"How many bags?"

There was the briefest pause before Max answered, "Four."

"My report was to expect five. You lose one?"

"No, sir. There were four."

Again a pause, and then Kaufman's voice, cold, steely. "You'd better be telling the truth. I'll find out."

The room above was as silent as a graveyard. Not a chair creaked. Not a foot moved.

Dena was stunned. What kind of meeting was this? It reminded her of TV movies about crime syndicates. Kaufman sounded like the head man, the boss of this group. But he was Guy's uncle!

Kaufman's voice spoke again. "Next business. Paul Roth. I don't trust him."

Dena held her breath. She was afraid to guess what happened to people Kaufman didn't trust.

15

The Merlins

The light outdoors was becoming dim and in the cellar it was already night. A night of terror.

Dena and Barney sat motionless on the bench by the window.

Besides the constant fear that someone might climb down through the trapdoor and discover them, they were tortured by mosquitoes that had come into the cellar through the open window. They didn't dare to slap the insects or even scratch the itching welts.

Dena longed to climb out the window and run far away from the schoolhouse and the mosquitoes and the ruthless man in the room above. What would Gramp think of the kind and generous Kaufman if he could hear him now?

"We'll use Roth for the pickup tomorrow," said Kaufman. "And that's the last time. He knows too much."

Again there was silence. Then Kaufman added, "Max, you take care of him."

"Right," said Max.

"Don't bungle the job like you did with Sebastian's boat," warned Kaufman.

Dena was stiff with horror. Kaufman sounded like a businessman giving directions to his secretary. Was it possible he was talking about killing Paul?

A new voice asked, "You going to stop Operation Pickup?" Dena thought she recognized the voice of the man who ran the lobster car. Although Maryann Kosac had written that new people owned the store and lobster car, it was a surprise to find out that the man who bought their lobsters was in Kaufman's gang.

Kaufman answered, "Certainly not. It's too profitable. You'll find me a replacement for Roth. This is only the beginning. We're in the perfect spot for importing—stolen art, jewels, fugitives who want to get into this country."

The cold, calm voice went on. "Soon Merlins will control the entire island. We—must—get—Sebastian's—land!" He emphasized each word. "The old man has the best harbor on the island and it faces east where our deliveries come from."

Merlins? thought Dena. What was that all about? Did these crooks have the nerve to think they were magicians like the good Merlin in the King Arthur legends?

Another person spoke up. It was the man who ran the store. So the storekeeper was in with Kaufman, too. "Walter tranquilized that dog, but good," he said. "So we won't have no trouble torching the cabin."

"Wait about the cabin," snapped Kaufman. "It may not be necessary. We could use that house."

So Walter was the one who had killed Hector. And just as they had guessed, he had used a tranquilizer.

Dena felt sick. She couldn't bear to stay in the cellar another minute. But when she tugged at Barney's arm, he shook his head.

If he wouldn't go, then she would go alone. She stood up and took a step toward the dim oblong of the window. The toe of her sneaker caught on a broken place in the floor, causing a loose piece of cement to roll over with a noise that sounded to Dena like an avalanche.

Dena froze. She heard Barney catch his breath. In the schoolroom all was quiet. How well could they hear cellar noises?

When at last someone spoke, Dena sank back onto the bench.

Barney was right. As long as they sat still, they were safer here than they would be if they climbed out the window. For all they knew, a lookout might be posted outside. Or someone might glance out and see them. And that would be the end.

Dena leaned her head back against the cold stone of the cellar wall and tried to forget the mosquitoes. Someplace she had read that you could bear pain if you thought hard enough about something else.

Overhead the meeting continued. Listening, Dena soon forgot the mosquitoes in her alarm at what she was hearing.

Again and again she heard the word "Merlin." She began to be sure that the men upstairs belonged to a crime ring called Merlin.

They were making plans to continue the smuggling. Arrangements were being made with a connection in South America.

Someone asked in a cautious tone, "What about your nephew? He acts kinda cozy with Paul's stepdaughter. That could lead to trouble."

Kaufman answered sharply, "I've taken care of that."

"I told you all along he's too young," said the other voice.

"You're wrong. His age makes him perfect. Who'd suspect a teenage kid with a gym bag?"

So that was why Guy hadn't phoned the day after the picnic. Kaufman had forbidden it. And it also explained his coolness on the telephone. Probably his uncle had been listening. However, Guy had stopped at the house today. Had he decided not to obey his uncle?

Dena wondered how Paul had gotten mixed up with a gang like this. As for Guy, Kaufman was his uncle, so it was natural that he would be involved. But it was a bitter disappointment that Guy was working with these cruel men. Would he become a killer some day?

In the room above, chairs scraped back. The men began to move around. Someone walked to the rear of the room and stopped near the trapdoor. Was he going to open it?

No, the footsteps moved away toward the front of the building. Everyone seemed to be leaving. Dena could even hear the *puff!* as the lamps were blown out. The key turned in the lock and the Merlins descended the front steps. She and Barney continued to remain motionless until the sound of voices faded away in the distance.

Finally Barney whispered, "Let's go."

He offered his knee as a step and helped her out the window. Then she held it open for him while he scrambled out.

They flattened themselves against the wall and listened, but all was hushed except the wind in the maples and pines and the roll of the sea.

Without a word they cut south across the narrow strip of meadow to the spruce woods. There they stopped to make sure no one was following them.

Barney scouted a few paces into the woodland. "It's too dark to go through here without a light."

"But it's too bright on the cliff path," objected Dena. The moon, high overhead, bleached the meadow and shimmered on the ocean.

"Let's follow the edge of the woods," said Barney. "We can stay in the shadow."

Once they were out of sight of the school they dared to walk more slowly, but they still spoke in whispers. If anyone saw them they would assume they were a pair of lovers, thought Dena.

"I'll have to tell Paul," she said. "I think they're planning to kill him."

Barney asked fearfully, "D'you think he'll tell Kaufman we were in the cellar? It sounds as if he's one of the gang, even if he is in trouble with them."

"I don't think he'll tell, but I'll have to risk it, because if I don't, they'll get him sure. I won't mention that you were with me."

"Why not? I'm in this as deep as you. I'm glad we listened. Now I'm sure Kaufman's behind all of Gramp's trouble," Barney said. "The man in Bangor who keeps trying to buy Gramp's land must be a Merlin."

Lights were on at home and Dena could see Paul at the telephone.

"Want to come in?" asked Dena.

"No. Gramp will be looking for me. At least I can tell him Hector didn't suffer." He lifted his hand in a half salute. "Take care."

Dena's mother met her at the back door. "Thank goodness you're home! We called Gramp and he told us you and Barney left before he got home, and that was a long time ago."

Paul came into the kitchen. "Where have you been?" he demanded.

"I have to tell you something," said Dena. She looked from one to the other. "It's important."

Paul studied her face. "Does it have anything to do with the way you and Barney feel about each other?"

"No."

He moved toward the back door. "Let's go out where it's cooler."

That's funny, thought Dena.

Her mother protested, "It's plenty cool in here." But Paul put his arm around her and walked her onto the porch. "Not cool enough for me."

When they were in the back yard, he pulled three lawn chairs close together and sat down in one of them. "Now tell us," he said. "I think I know."

"Why'd you bring us out here?" asked Dena.

"You're first."

So Dena told him of her long vigil in the cellar of the old schoolhouse, leaving out nothing except the fact that Barney had been with her. She even told him about finding the bag of heroin.

When she had finished, she said, "I had to let you know, Paul, so you could get away."

"You're taking a chance telling me, aren't you, Dena?" he asked.

"Yes."

"Then why did you do it?"

"Because I don't want you to get killed."

Paul said, "Good. Now I think it's time for me to level with you and Janet. I brought you out here to

talk because I believe the house is bugged and someone hears every word we say inside."

"Oh, Paul!" Dena's mother had been sitting with
clenched hands. "Why?"

"Because Kaufman doesn't trust me, and he has
good reason not to. I've been spying on him and his
gang."

Dena felt a weight lift from her chest. Paul wasn't a
criminal. Better yet, he was fighting against the Merlins.

"I'm not surprised I'm in trouble with Kaufman,"
Paul said. "I knew I was on shaky ground when he
sent Max here to go through my desk the other day."

"Oh, that's who it was!" Dena was surprised. "But
he walked so heavy, and Max is tall and thin."

"I know, but he's heavy footed. He's awkward and
comes down hard with every step. When you told
how the fellow sounded, I knew it must be Max."

Dena's mother was trembling. "Why did you get
into this, Paul? It's so dangerous."

He put his arm around her. "I thought it seemed
like a good idea. You don't want these Merlins taking
over our island, do you?"

"No, but I don't want you getting killed, either!"

"Some things are worth taking a risk," said Paul.
"Like cutting down on the flow of hard drugs into our
high school." So that was Paul's real reason for tan-
gling with the Merlins, thought Dena.

"Paul," she asked, "why do they call themselves

Merlins? Do they think they're—sorcerers?"

"Possibly, but a merlin is also a bird of prey. We call it a pigeon hawk, but actually it's a small falcon. The English call it a merlin."

"A bird of prey," said Dena. "That fits." She reached into her sweater pocket. "I found this paper in the wastebasket at the school. There's a drawing of a bird on it, like a hawk. Maybe it's a merlin."

"Let's see it." Paul took the small piece of paper to the kitchen. When he came back he returned it to Dena. "That's intended to be a merlin, all right, though I'm not sure I'd recognize it if the word 'merlin' hadn't been printed under it. Better save that paper. It's another piece of evidence."

Dena pocketed the drawing. "Did you know the Merlins were smuggling heroin?"

"Yes, though I couldn't prove it. Max never gave me a chance to check the contents of those plastic bags." The moonlight was bright enough so Dena could see his smile as he said, "I saw you and Barney when you found that bag the other day, and then the Drug Enforcement Administration told me about the package Gramp took to the police."

Dena reproached him. "And you didn't let on!"

Paul said, "I wasn't ready to tell you what I was working on. But now with the information you and Gramp have, plus what I've learned, we can set the trap. I'll go out with Max tomorrow morning. And by the way, he phoned tonight. The pickup is at eight o'clock."

His wife groaned. "Must you go?"

"Yes, but it'll be the last time. The day after to-morrow we should be able to catch Kaufman with the heroin in his possession. I'll call the DEA."

"You take it all so calmly," she complained. "You talk as if it's a—ball game!"

"I've had more time to get used to it, hon," said Paul.

"But why did you take Max out in your boat when you knew he was smuggling?" she asked.

"Because I wanted to get proof. Right from the start I was suspicious of Max and the fellow he worked with. They wouldn't go out for days, and then they'd go way out, even when the weather was foul. Never got many lobsters. Then one day when I was hauling a good distance out I saw a big yacht slow down as it passed Max's boat. I took a long look through the glasses—and I saw Max latch onto one of those plastic bags with his gaff hook."

"Why'd you think it was drugs in the bags?" asked Dena.

"I had a hunch. I'd read about a similar operation in Florida. So I got friendly with Max and made him think I'd do anything for money. I was in luck because about that time Kaufman was desperate for someone to help Max pick up the bags—preferably someone who was a lobsterman with a boat. The fellow he had before had an unfortunate accident and fell overboard. Never seen again."

Dena shuddered. "Don't let that happen to you. Did they pay you for running the boat?"

"They kept putting it off and I didn't press them. I couldn't keep the money, anyway."

"But Paul—" Dena was still eagerly working her way through the maze. "How do you know you can catch Kaufman with the heroin day after tomorrow?"

"Because I've found out how he operates. Max keeps the heroin till the day the mailboat comes. Then he takes it to Kaufman early in the morning. So the stuff is in Kaufman's hands from then until Guy carries it to the mailboat. I've watched them from the tower. That's why I wanted the tower room, Dena, so I could keep track of the Merlins."

"I was afraid Guy was carrying the stuff," said Dena sadly. "I'm sure I saw him exchange bags with a man in the Harbor Coffee Shop the day before I came home."

"It's too bad. Guy's a good kid. But I'm afraid he's caught in his uncle's web. His uncle's as bad as they come. He's a madman, if you ask me."

"But he gave all that money for the generator and the roads," Dena reminded him.

"That was smart. He's trying to keep on the good side of the old-timers. Even if he gets control of the island, he needs to have some genuine lobstermen stay here as a cover for his activities."

Paul stood up and stretched. "I'll run over to

Gramp's now and phone the DEA. Can't trust our phone, you know."

"You keep talking about the DEA," said Dena's mother. "Are they working with you on this?"

"Yes. I contacted them as soon as I began to suspect Kaufman, about a month ago. One of their men gave a talk at school last winter. Remember, hon?"

"Yes," his wife replied. "But you never told me about all this."

"I wanted to," said Paul. "Oh, how I wanted to! But I thought it was safer for you not to know. And you'd have worried about it."

"I certainly would. I'm worried now, but it's better than not knowing. After this," she said seriously, "I don't want to be sheltered from the truth as if I were a child."

Paul seemed taken aback. "I see. Guess I haven't been fair. I know you two can take it, and I'm glad I have you to help me through the next couple of days. I wish they were over." He put his hand on Dena's shoulder. "I keep reminding myself that in about two months we'll all be in Gullport High School, too busy to even remember our tangle with the underworld."

Dena looked up at his shadowy face. His words answered the question that had been bothering her. They would all be together this winter. A family.

Not even the menace of the Merlins could overshadow her joy at being accepted by Paul.

16

Escape Plan

Paul left at seven the next morning.

Dena heard him go and wearily crawled out of bed. She had been up until late the night before, but she knew her mother might need companionship during the lonely hours ahead.

Mrs. Roth was sitting at the kitchen table, sipping coffee and staring into space. Her face lighted up when she saw Dena.

"You didn't have to get up, dear," she said. "But I'm glad to see you."

Dena shook cereal into a bowl and poured herself a glass of orange juice. "Let's go outside," she suggested. "It's a nice morning."

They sat at the round table that stood on the small flagstone terrace at the foot of the porch steps.

"I'll be glad when this house is unbugged," said Mrs. Roth.

Dena laughed. "This way we get more fresh air. Mom, we ought to do something special today."

Her mother shook her head. "I just want to stay

here and wait for him." She put down her cup. "I've been trying to figure out why I didn't realize what Paul was doing."

"Actually," said Dena, "there wasn't much for you to notice. He went lobstering as usual and when he was in the tower, how could you know he wasn't watching birds?"

"He really is writing a book on our island birds. I've read part of it."

"Maybe I can have my room back now," said Dena.

Her mother looked across at her and smiled. "I'm sure you can. And I have an idea what we can do today. Let's clean house, beginning at the top."

Three hours later Dena was dusting the dining-room furniture when she heard someone coming up the back steps. She looked through the window and saw Paul.

"Mom!" she screamed. "He's home!"

She dropped her duster and ran outdoors and flung her arms around her stepfather.

He hugged her and patted her back. "How about a mug-up? I'm starved."

They were eating an early lunch when Guy came to the back door.

"Come in. Pull up a chair and join us," Paul said.

"No, thanks." Guy was out of breath and his face was wet with perspiration. "I just want to see Dena."

Dena went to the door. "What's up, Guy?"

"I have to talk with you. Come outside. Please."

Was this a trap? Dena gave Paul a questioning glance. He nodded slightly, so Dena opened the screen door and followed Guy down the steps.

He led the way toward the shore at a fast pace, but instead of going to the cliff as Dena expected, he stopped in the heart of the spruce woods.

"I've got to tell you something!" He seemed frantic. "We have to get Paul off the island!"

"Why?"

"Just take my word for it."

Dena turned away. As much as she liked him, how could she trust a boy who worked with criminals? "I'm not taking your word for anything. Probably your uncle sent you."

Guy ran after her and blocked her way. "What do you know?"

Dena stopped and looked at him with blazing eyes. Suddenly she forgot to be careful. "Quite a lot. I was at the meeting last night."

"Sure you were," he said scornfully.

She had blown it already, so she might as well finish the job. "I was in the cellar and I heard the whole thing. Max and Paul made a pickup today. So I suppose you're going to Gullport on the *Henrietta* tomorrow."

"No, I'm not. And I don't have time to argue. My uncle's at the harbor and I have to get home before he does. Listen! Max will come after Paul this afternoon about two o'clock. He'll tell him they have to go on another pickup right away. And if Paul goes he'll never come back."

Dena tried to sound calm. "So Paul can refuse to go."

Guy drew in his breath sharply. "It won't do any good. They'll get him another way. Soon."

"How do you know all this?" demanded Dena.

"Max told me. I was just at his house. I didn't want him to know I was coming here so I went home and then sneaked back through the woods."

Dena felt faint. "Can't you stop him?"

"I tried. But he says it's Paul's life or his. You don't say no to my uncle."

Dena asked suspiciously, "How come Max told you?"

"Because we're friends and he had to talk to someone. He feels bad about having to kill Paul because he likes him. And he never killed anyone before." Guy paced away and peered between the trees as if afraid of being overheard. He came back and seized Dena's arm. "Please! Believe me! Paul has to get away fast. I have a plan. He can take my boat."

Dena felt an agony of doubt. "Why should he take your boat when he has one of his own?"

"Because they won't let him use his own boat!" Guy seemed to be struggling to control his impatience. "Walter's watching it now."

"He can fly, then."

"No! My uncle has a Merlin running the plane. You have to believe me. This is the only way!"

Dena said fiercely, "How can I trust you when I know you work for your uncle? He may have sent you here."

"Look, I delivered his goods twice. He convinced me I owed it to him for all he did for me. But I'm through. I knew he was in some kind of crooked work, but I didn't know how bad it was. When I found out he had Hector killed, that opened my eyes. And now, Paul . . ."

So some good had come from Hector's death, thought Dena.

Guy seemed rooted to the ground in front of her. His expression became shy and yet fiercely honest. "I said Hector's death made me realize how bad my uncle is. But actually, knowing you made the biggest difference. The day of our picnic I made up my mind I was going to break away from Uncle Earl."

Dena met his eyes with equal honesty. "I'm glad. Thanks for telling me. Will your uncle let you quit?"

"He'll fight it, but I don't think he'd kill me." He thought a moment. "Maybe he would. My aunt's afraid for her life. Anyway, I'd rather die than belong to the Merlins."

She came to a decision. "I'll get Paul."

"No!" Guy was more frantic than ever. "I've stayed too long now. Tell him to meet me at that bay at the south end of the island—Tom Thumb Bay—at half past one." Guy whipped around and disappeared among the trees.

Dena ran back toward the house, but she had not gone far when Paul stepped from behind a bushy spruce.

"Your bodyguard at your service," he said.

"Did you hear what Guy said?"

"Most of it."

"Do you think we can trust him? Seems funny Max would tell him he's going to kill you."

"We don't have much choice." Paul walked slowly, thinking out loud. "Anyway, I'm inclined to believe him. Max has been friendly all along. He may have hoped Guy would tell us about the plan so we could get away."

Dena pulled at his arm. "Come on! You don't have time to poke along!"

He followed her toward the house. "What makes you think I'm going without you and your mother?"

"We're not the ones they want to kill."

He was unmoved. "I'm not going alone. How do I know what Kaufman and his men might do to you? If they suspect you're onto them, they'll try to put you out of the way."

No matter what Dena and her mother said, Paul remained firm.

"You can make better speed in the boat without us," said Dena. Again they were talking on the little terrace behind the house.

Her mother added, "And someone may be watching and get suspicious if we all leave."

"We won't go at the same time." Paul looked at his watch. "It's almost one o'clock now. I'll go to Gramp's and phone the DEA about our change in plans. You two follow in five minutes, and don't take the cliff path. I'll see you at Tom Thumb Bay at one-thirty."

"But we might get held up," said his wife. "Paul, when Guy gets there, you go!"

He kissed her. "I'll leave when you and Dena arrive on the scene. By the way, no extra clothes, just a jacket. And you might carry a basket, as if you were going out for strawberries."

Paul picked up his binoculars from the round table and slung them around his neck. "I'm going to check out a few birds." He waved and was soon out of sight.

In five minutes Dena and her mother started down the road, making no effort to stay hidden.

"If the Merlins see us sneaking through the woods they'll be suspicious," Mrs. Roth had said. "Better to act natural."

Dena hoped they looked like a mother and daughter going berrying, but she felt as if they were center stage with a spotlight glaring on them. Since Kaufman was so determined to get rid of Paul, it wasn't likely that he'd let any of Paul's family leave the island, especially if he guessed they were a danger to him.

When they passed the store, her mother's friend, Vi Hazlett, came out with a bag of groceries.

"Going berrying?" she called. "You're headed the wrong way, Janet. Lots of strawberries up at the point." She jerked her head toward the north.

Mrs. Roth answered with a stiff smile. "Thanks, Vi. We'll try there next."

Guy's boat, looking too small for the company it kept, was still at its mooring near Earl Kaufman's cruiser. Someone was working on the cruiser, but Guy's boat was empty. Where was Guy? He should be starting soon.

The spruce woods were ahead. It seemed strange to enter the green shade with fear prickling the back of her neck. Now that she knew what danger was, Dena wondered that she had always taken safety for granted.

No one else seemed to be on the path that wound through the woodland. Yet, even if it were thronged with people, she would still expect an attacker to leap from the shadows and aim directly for her and her mother. At one moment her imagination conjured up a dim figure that looked like Frank with his blond curls, and seconds later she drew back from a ghost with Walter's skillful footwork.

When they emerged from the woods the light on

the airfield was dazzling. Dena felt even more exposed to the unseen eyes that she was sure were following them.

Is this what it's like to be a hunted animal? she wondered.

She stole a look at Gramp's log house, standing solid and friendly to the east of the airstrip.

"I don't see anyone at Gramp's," she said.

"I know. I looked, too." Her mother leaned down and pushed aside the grass. "Vi's right. I don't see any berries. Wait. There are a few over here."

Dena giggled shakily. "I'd rather run than pick." She forced herself to walk slowly, to bend and pluck a berry now and then. They mustn't act as if they were in a hurry to get anyplace.

They worked their way along the airfield, skirting Gramp's pond where a few ducks rose squawking. They seemed to shout to all the island, "Here they are!"

Dena led the way onto the path to the bay. It followed the stream that flowed south from the duck pond. Stillness closed around them. Gradually Dena began to hear the orchestration of silence, the buzz of a honeybee and the whine of mosquitoes. Every now and then a bird sang a few notes. A frog said, "*Ka-chunk!*"

Halfway between the pond and the bay they reached a thicket of blackberry bushes that had overgrown the path.

"Here's where we wade," said Dena in a hoarse whisper. "Take off your sneakers, Mom."

They rolled their dungarees above their knees and stepped into the cold water of the stream. We're on a hike, Dena told herself. Mom and I've always had fun prowling around the island. But it was no use trying to fool herself. It wasn't fun. Her mother's eyes were too bright and when she touched her daughter's arm, her hand was clammy.

Dena tried to encourage her. "We're almost there."

A fresh breeze announced that the ocean was near. They rounded a bend in the stream and ahead of them was small, quiet Tom Thumb Bay where Dena had sometimes fished or taken a swim in the chilly water. Gulls sat on the semicircle of rocks that jutted out from shore.

Dena looked at her watch. One thirty-five. Neither Paul nor Guy was here. She had been sure Guy would be on time. Already he was five minutes late. Had he run into trouble?

"I wonder where Paul is," murmured Mrs. Roth.

Dena lifted a cautioning finger to her lips. The voice of the stream had a changed sound. A bush rustled and a crow shot into the air with a startled caw.

Someone was coming toward them. She stared helplessly up stream, hoping that the person who was coming was Paul.

17

Pursued!

What if the approaching person were Frank or Walter? Dena edged back into the bushes that grew close to the stream and pulled her mother with her. There they crouched side by side, waiting.

The splashing sounds came nearer, stopped.

Paul's voice spoke quietly, "Janet? Dena?"

Mrs. Roth leaped from her hiding place. Paul beamed and held out his arms.

He looked as if he were enjoying himself. His red hair and beard shone in the sun. Dena could understand why her mother had been attracted to him.

"Did you talk to the DEA?" she heard her mother whisper.

"Yep. They're coming out to meet us. The Coast Guard's bringing them." Paul nodded toward the bay. "No sign of Guy?"

Dena shook her head.

"I hope his uncle didn't get wise to him," said Paul. He climbed out of the stream onto a large rock. Like Dena and her mother, he was barefooted and carrying his sneakers. "Man! That's cold water!"

"Did anyone see you come?" Mrs. Roth asked.

"Not that I know of. Barney said Walter was hanging around the wharf, but I don't believe he saw me. I went into Gramp's on the airstrip side."

Dena worried. "I hope Gramp and Barney are safe."

"I don't think Kaufman will move against Gramp till he gets me out of the way." Paul stopped and tilted his head as if listening, then waded upstream a few paces. Dena watched him with alarm.

Soon he came back. "Thought I heard something."

"You do," said Dena, relieved. She had just caught the sound of a motorboat approaching from the west.

Paul bent low and ran to the cover of the bushes near the mouth of the stream. After looking intently toward the bay, he stood up and waved his hand over his head.

"It's Guy!" he called. "And he's alone."

Until this moment Dena had not realized how afraid she had been that he might not come. Guy maneuvered his boat as close to shore as possible, then climbed out.

Dena, wading toward him, looked up and met his eyes. They seemed a brighter blue than ever. "We're all going," she told him. "Paul won't leave without us."

"I don't blame him," Guy said. "Sorry I was late. I had a rough time getting away. My uncle's going to

Gullport with the horse this afternoon and I had to get his waterproof jacket from Max's house and find his sunglasses."

With the *horse?* Of course, the heroin.

"Watch out for him," warned Guy. "You know that sea anemone you told me about that paralyzes its prey and stuffs them in its mouth?"

"Yes."

"That's Uncle Earl. He looks good, but he's a killer."

Paul was already at the wheel. While Dena and her mother climbed aboard, Guy, still in the water, gave him quick directions on operating the boat and ship-to-shore radio.

He let go his hold on the gunwale. "I'm going back and try to keep Uncle Earl from leaving too soon."

"He'll want to know where your boat is," Dena warned.

Guy reassured her. "I'll tell him I ran out of gas and had to beach it." He started away, then turned back. "Don't worry. You have plenty of gas." He looked directly at Dena. "Good luck!"

Dena watched him wade toward the beach. He was halfway there when a movement on shore caught her eye. To her horror, she glimpsed Frank's yellow curls, partially hidden by the bushes. She'd know that dandelion head anyplace.

An instant later he was gone, running up the stream.

Had Guy betrayed them?

But apparently Frank's arrival was also a surprise to Guy. He backed away from the shore, then whirled around and splashed toward the boat as fast as he could. Dena helped him aboard.

Paul slid away from the wheel. "Take it, Guy."

Guy vaulted over the back of the seat. Seconds later the boat leaped forward and roared out of Tom Thumb Bay.

"Which way?" asked Guy.

"Due west."

"Might hit land sooner if we go northwest."

"I know," said Paul. "But the DEA will be looking for us on the way to Gullport."

"The DEA?" echoed Guy. "Then they already know?"

"The whole thing."

Dena wondered how Guy felt about that. She and her mother sat opposite each other on seats built on either side of the open cockpit.

Paul handed Dena the binoculars. "Let us know the minute you spot Kaufman. He's sure to follow us, now that Frank has seen us."

Soon Sebastian Island was behind them. The sea, a darker blue than the sky, was deserted save for the cormorants and gulls and a few distant ships. Once Dena thought she saw a seal.

Guy kept a fast speed and a straight course. Dena admired his control of the boat.

In half an hour, land appeared to the north. They were going to make it.

But ten minutes later Dena saw a motion, a mere speck in the direction of Sebastian Island.

With a sick feeling, she studied it through the glasses. "Boat coming from the east," she told Paul.

He came back and took the binoculars. "Looks like Kaufman's cruiser." Paul returned to Guy. "I think your uncle's on the way. What'll he do?"

"Try to sink us."

"Will he use a gun?"

"Might. But he's big on accidents. Figures that way no one can pin anything on him."

Paul groaned. "I hope the Coast Guard gets here before Kaufman does! Let's give them a call."

"My uncle will be listening."

"Yeah. Well, we'd better call anyway. You make the contact. You're the operator."

Dena could see Guy talking on the ship-to-shore radio. After a few words, he turned it over to Paul. She couldn't hear the conversation.

Paul turned around. "They're well on the way. You both have life jackets on?"

"No."

"Well, get 'em on! We may need them when Kaufman gets here." Paul took a jacket and helped Guy into one.

The boat approaching from the east was rapidly gaining on them.

153

"Can you get more speed out of this?" asked Paul.

"Nope. I tried, but this is as fast as it'll go."

Dena kept the binoculars to her eyes. It was Kaufman's boat, without a doubt. She recognized its lines, especially the sharp forward thrust of the bow.

How big it looked! She no longer needed the glasses to see Kaufman in the bow. Frank was towering beside him with his blond hair streaming back in the wind. She recalled that when she had seen him trimming the grass around Kaufmans' patio she had thought he looked like an amiable bear.

Right now the friendly bear had something in his hand and he seemed to be pointing it at them.

Ping!

Dena heard a sharp, whining noise and saw a spurt of water leap up beside the boat. She had a feeling of unreality. Was he shooting at *them?*

"Duck!" shouted Guy.

Dena and her mother hit the green carpet.

Another shot sounded and Guy began to zigzag. Dena lifted her head enough to see that Paul was crouched beside his seat, talking on the radiotelephone.

The cruiser was close behind.

For several minutes nothing happened. Looking back over her shoulder, Dena saw that Kaufman in the bow of the cruiser had a megaphone in his hand.

His voice reached her ears with such force she realized the megaphone must be electronic. "Stop or we'll fire!" he shouted.

In answer Guy swerved away.

Good! thought Dena. We can't give in to Kaufman. We can't trust him.

Guy shouted, "Get behind the end of the seats. Up here!"

Dena and her mother crawled forward and sat down behind the end of the built-in seats with their heads between their knees. At any moment Dena expected to hear another shot, or worse yet, to feel one.

Guy poured on the speed and steered straight ahead.

At first Kaufman's boat did not follow and there was no gunfire.

Paul looked back. "They're talking. Wonder why they don't shoot?"

"I told you," said Guy. "He'll try for an accident. The shooting was to stop us, but we didn't bite."

Suddenly Kaufman's boat seemed to leap forward. It came directly at them like a torpedo.

"Watch out!" yelled Paul. "They're going to ram us!"

"Tell me when!" shouted Guy.

Dena braced herself and kept her head down. Her mother was doing the same.

"Now!" cried Paul.

Guy reacted with a quick turn of the wheel that sent Dena and her mother sprawling. Kaufman's boat passed them, missing by a foot.

At once the cruiser circled, obviously intending to return for another strike.

"He's coming!" shouted Paul.

Again Kaufman's boat missed, but this time by inches.

The small craft was more maneuverable, but the cruiser had more speed. How long before Kaufman would connect?

Sooner or later they'll get us, thought Dena. But at least Guy's making it hard for them.

She prepared for another attack. Seconds passed. Kaufman was taking his time. Making sure this one counted?

Dena had her head down and her eyes closed. Paul's voice cut in.

"Hang in there!" he called. "Help's coming!"

Dena straightened up and looked ahead through the windshield. A white boat was coming toward them at a speed that sent foam curling up and out from the bow like the horns of a monstrous ram. Above and in front of the white boat was a helicopter.

Dena spun around to look for Kaufman's boat but already it had turned due north. The helicopter and Coast Guard cutter followed. Guy set his course to join them.

By the time they reached the scene, Kaufman's boat was halted with the cutter alongside it. Men from the Coast Guard boat had already boarded

Kaufman's cruiser. The helicopter was hovering to one side.

Through the binoculars Dena recognized Frank, Walter, and Max on Kaufman's boat. They were turning over their weapons to a tall man in civilian dress. Two men in the light-blue dungaree uniform of the Coast Guard stood nearby with guns trained on the three Merlins.

Dena gave the glasses to Paul. "I don't see Kaufman."

Then she saw a slight figure with blond hair come onto the deck. Even without the glasses she recognized Kaufman by the way he moved, with the speed and precision of a well-built machine.

He ran to the bow, away from the other men. He was carrying the blue canvas bag. As he raced toward the rail he pulled back the zipper.

"Stop him!" Dena screamed even though she knew it was useless. With the rush of the water and the beat of the helicopter, the men on the cruiser couldn't hear her.

A crisp voice from the helicopter came over the loud-speaker in tones that carried even to Guy's boat. "Stop where you are or I'll shoot that bag out of your hand!"

Kaufman faltered and looked up.

In that moment a thin, hunched figure darted toward Kaufman. It was Max! He wrestled the bag from him and handed it to the man in civilian dress.

Paul had been watching as closely as Dena. "That's Special Agent Reichert from the DEA," he said. "The tall one. I've met him several times. I'm glad they caught Kaufman with the heroin."

"Would it have ruined the whole case if he'd gotten rid of it?" asked Dena.

"No. But I'd say this makes it airtight."

Mrs. Roth said, "I should think he'd have tossed it overboard before this."

"You don't know my uncle," said Guy. "Money's everything to him, and he told me that stuff is worth a lot."

"About a million dollars," said Paul.

Suddenly Dena's attention was drawn back to the deck of the cruiser. Kaufman had made another dash for the rail.

"He's climbing over!" she cried.

Special Agent Reichert seized Kaufman's coat as he went over and held him until Max and the two Coast Guardsmen joined him. It took all of them to pull the furious little man back onto the deck.

Paul was right, thought Dena. Kaufman has gone mad.

A week later Dena was in her tower room putting on her best blue and pink shirt. Tonight she and her mother and Paul were giving a party, a cookout in the back yard. Barney and Gramp were coming, and so were Guy and his Aunt Irene. Only Hector, dear

Hector, wouldn't be there. How he would have enjoyed the handouts—the bits of hamburger and hot dog—and all the patting he'd have gotten!

Paul and Dena had spoken for Guy, and he had been released in his aunt's care. He still faced charges for acting as a courier for his uncle, but the DEA had promised to speak to the judge in his favor.

"I doubt if we'd have been alive if it weren't for Guy O'Neill," Paul had told Special Agent Reichert. "And Max Collier—well, I have hopes for him. He's willing to testify against the Merlins."

"You did a great job," Reichert told Paul.

Dena remembered with pride how Paul had put his arm around her and said, "I have to admit I had a lot of help from my girl."

Dena heard a shout from the yard below. When she ran to the window she saw Gramp and Barney looking up at her and waving. Barney was carrying something. Something small and alive and wriggling.

Dena waved back and raced downstairs to meet them. There was going to be a basset hound at the cookout, after all.